50¢ FOR 3 DAYS 10¢ EACH ADD'L DAY

MAIN LINE KILL

The city holds enough secrets to keep a private detective busy. So when Leverton walks into the office with a fantastic story of sudden death on a commuter train, investigator Maxwell Daly advises him to tell his story to the police, for he has no wish to get involved in a murder case. Then Leverton is found with the top of his head blown off in what appears to be the shooting suicide of an eternal triangle involving pretty socialite Carol Morden.

Maxwell Daly remembers the dead man's words and sets out to find the truth. Slowly he puts together a complicated jigsaw of death, drugs and greed, whose pieces lie locked in a plush Birmingham nightclub run by an American gangster, and in the grimy hands of the beatnik fraternity.

BUSBY AND HOLTHAM

Main Line Kill

Walker and Company   New York

Copyright © 1968 by ROGER BUSBY AND GERALD HOLTHAM.

All rights reserved. No part of this book may be reproduced or transmitted in any form or by any means, electronic or mechanical, including photocopying, recording, or by any information storage and retrieval system, without permission in writing from the Publisher.

All the characters and events portrayed in this story are fictitious.

First published in the United States of America in 1968 by Walker and Company, a division of the Walker Publishing Company, Inc.

Library of Congress Catalog Card Number: 68-30945

Printed in the United States of America from type set in Great Britain.

MAIN LINE KILL

1

Four minutes late, the train came sidling noiselessly into the station. Leverton had no difficulty in finding an empty compartment almost a carriage length from the one he had seen Battersby enter. He did not know whether the man had seen him or not, but he had taken care not to advertise his presence. With a sigh he released himself into his seat and waited for the train to move.

Presently it began to pull away. The platform slid past, its crenellated roof rippling backwards faster and faster as the carriage ran out into the mid-morning sunlight. Before long Leverton began to feel hot in the compartment and, as the countryside blurred by, he felt the warning stabs that preceded his migraine. It was certainly going to be a long day. A couple of stations came and went as the diesel threaded its way through the city's suburban sprawl and Leverton, still alone in the compartment, decided he would have to take some tablets before the pain became unbearable. He got up and was making his way down the corridor with a conscious effort when the train plunged into a tunnel.

After a second's delay the lights came on, just as Leverton neared the end of the corridor and passed Battersby's compartment. Battersby was sitting in the far corner by the window. There were two men in raincoats sitting opposite him and he seemed to be talking to them. None of the three looked into the corridor, and Leverton glanced hurriedly away and continued to the small toilet and washroom. He let the cold water run on to his wrist for several seconds, then took two of the little white pills, gulping them down with a handful of water, and waited for the pain in his head to subside. Afterwards he was feeling much better and leaned against the sway of the train as he opened the brown door. The throbbing of the diesel dropped to a continuous note as it freewheeled into another station and jolted to a standstill. Leverton had reached

Battersby's compartment again when the train began to move off and he couldn't resist a quick glance inside. Battersby was alone now and seemed to be asleep in the corner seat. His eyes were closed, his mouth open and his hat was across his chest.

Suddenly the train lurched, slowed and began to accelerate again, making Leverton grip the rail across the corridor window to retain his balance. The effect on Battersby was even more marked. His body creased from the waist and tipped forward. Then he slithered soundlessly off the seat on to the narrow floor.

Leverton looked on foolishly, his mouth agape. Through the far window of the compartment the platform was sliding away. The train passed the large brown and cream smut-stained nameboard of Tyseley station, and it passed two men in raincoats walking towards the exit.

Leverton came to himself, took a quick breath, and pulled open the compartment door. His mind a racing flywheel, he moved to where Battersby was lying face down. He put his hand on Battersby's shoulder and turned him over to see his face. There was a blue tint on the man's cheek. He was heavy, but Leverton got him on to his side and then noticed the crumpled hat on the floor. It looked an expensive hat and it was half-full of blood. In Battersby's chest there was a large hole where the burnt clothing and shattered flesh clung sickeningly around a gaping wound. Leverton recoiled in horror and the body fell back to a prone position.

It was too much for Leverton. His mind a confusion, he slumped on to the seat in a state of shock. The next thing he could remember with any accuracy was the clattering bustle of New Street station shattering the spell. Impulsively he bolted for the corridor, left the train in a daze, and was three steps from the crowded security of the station forecourt when a porter checking the carriage found the body and yelled for him to stop.

Only a ticket collector barred Leverton's way at the

barrier. He panicked and hit the collector a sloppy blow on the chest, knocking him off balance. Then he sprinted out of the station entrance into the city street and managed to clamber on to a passing bus which was soon swallowed up in the traffic. The usual morbid crowds converged on the platform, hopeful of a macabre thrill, and the railway police who were the first officers on the scene were swamped in the crush. They took descriptions from the porter and ticket collector.

Fear gripped Leverton as he sat in the temporary safety of the crowded bus. He began to realize for the first time the appalling position he was in. He could be the suspect in a murder, the suspect they hunted down and printed photographs and descriptions of in the newspapers. He dismissed the idea of going straight to the police and telling them what had happened. They would never believe him, and then there was Carol Morden. She could link him with Battersby and it would look like the crime of a jealous lover. He was cornered and there was no way of escape. He was going to pay for a crime he had not committed, for the death of a man he knew he had hated and had secretly wished dead many times. Why did it have to happen to him? The bus stopped and Leverton was forced to leave his seat, no longer an anonymous passenger but already in his own mind a wanted murderer without a chance of clearing himself.

In that moment, Leverton groped wildly for something to help him. It could not end like that. It was too unfair. He was thinking about his wife and how badly he needed her help but could not ask for it. He saw again the faces of the lawyers in the divorce court, the judge and barristers in their wigs, the dark suits of the solicitors and their clerks. They would all be against him now. But there was one face . . . one face there in the court who was not one of them, one of the accusers. The man who had helped his wife. It was a long shot, but all Leverton had left was long shots.

2

Business had been fairly good just then and I was feeling a little mellow. I let Leverton tell his story without interruption. My office boasted about four bottles of the hard stuff and I only treated clients who looked very rich or very worried. I didn't see how Leverton could have looked more worried and I poured him some hospitality.

'So you were coming into town on your usual train and you saw a man from the same village killed by two men who got off the train at the station before New Street?' Leverton nodded. He was shaking although the whisky seemed to be calming him down a little. I didn't really think his story was very credible, but he had probably seen something and his imagination had done the rest.

'Assuming what you say is true, then you are withholding vital information from the police. The best thing you can do is report the whole thing straight away. If it will make you feel any better, I'll take you down to the station.' Leverton's eyes dilated and he began another fit of the shakes. From what I could remember of him he had not seemed a particularly nervous type and that made it all the more strange.

'You don't understand,' he said. 'Battersby . . . well the police will find out that I didn't like him. I mean he was going with Carol you know. She preferred him to me after all I had gone through for her . . . the divorce and everything. And then that bastard. . . .'

'Ever quarrelled with him in public?'

'Well, there have been scenes. . . .' he choked on the Scotch.

'That porter saw me . . . they'll know I didn't like Battersby—it'll be all over the village. I daren't face the police. You must help me. I didn't like it much when my wife hired you and you got her divorce with your evidence. I may have said some unpleasant things, but you knew what you were doing, you know your way around sordid things like this. I couldn't think... didn't know anyone else to ask. I can't tell the police. Look, I even hit that ticket collector.'

I grinned at the one compliment—I knew sordid things.

'There's nothing I can do,' I said. 'You will have to tell the police eventually. Do it now.'

He did not seem to appreciate the logic of that suggestion. 'Don't turn me away. I can't tell the police or even my solicitor. At least find out if they suspect me first. Perhaps you can tell them it wasn't me. I thought you would know what to do. Please don't turn me away!'

He had begun to gabble and his stubby fingers picked nervously at the buttons on his camel-hair overcoat. I felt quite sorry for Leverton at that moment and, if I could have thought of anything constructive which would have helped him, I would have probably done it. He was a pompous, flabby businessman who lived in a nice house in a dormitory village. His affair with Carol Morden had wrecked his marriage, and his life was in a mess.

'What do you want me to do? Give you a personal reference to the CID?' I said.

'As long as I stick to divorce, missing persons and the occasional civil case, the police think I'm all right. Crime is their province, and if I put my nose in, then I'm *persona non grata*.'

I was still not getting through to him. He seemed lost in his own thoughts for a second and then just muttered, 'Those killers. They saw me you know.'

'Look. See sense for God's sake. If you're in any danger then the only thing to do is to tell the police. I can't act as your personal bodyguard twenty-four hours a day. Now go straight down to the police headquarters, ask for Detective Chief Superintendent Grey and tell him all about it. I'll give you a lift if you like and introduce you.'

For all I knew, Leverton had killed the man himself and was trying to con me to help him get away. You can get quite a stretch for harbouring, and I had no intention of sampling Her Majesty's hospitality for anybody.

Leverton looked resigned, and very tired. 'If you won't help me. . . .'

'I'm helping you the best way possible,' I said. 'Let's go.'

He put his empty glass down on the desk, stood up, and looked down at me, shaking his head. 'I'll go alone. I don't need an escort thanks.'

I shrugged. 'All right, but for Pete's sake don't do anything foolish. Go to the police and tell them everything.' Leverton turned and opened the office door. His eyes fell on the square mahogany plaque on the corridor wall: Maxwell Daly. Investigations. But for his troubles he might well have looked ironical. Then he turned and was gone.

*

I sat and thought about the episode. After all that sort of thing doesn't happen every day, or every year for that matter. I hoped Leverton would go to the police, but I decided it was really none of my business, and it was not until the next morning that I had second thoughts.

I was back in my shabby little office with some letters to write before starting work for a woman with too much money and a wayward husband. First I looked at the post— two bills which I filed in the wastepaper basket. Then I glanced through the morning paper and got my first shock of the day. There were big headlines, two inches deep: 'Killing on city train', and below: 'Scientist dies from gunshots'.

The story related that Battersby had been shot in the stomach and chest with a large calibre pistol. The railway carriage had been taken off for forensic examination, and the police were asking for passengers on the train to come forward.

I began to write my letters after fighting down an impulse to telephone Leverton's home at Dukeswood. Then I went out and bought a lunch edition of the *Evening Mail* from the old newsvendor on the street corner. There was a lot of gingered up writing but no new facts on the killing. I didn't see the other story until I was back behind my desk. It was

6

just three inches on an inside page. Under the heading: 'Man dead at Dukeswood home', the story read: 'Police called to a Dukeswood house today found a local businessman dead from gunshot wounds. He was Mr William Leverton who lived alone following his recent divorce. A senior police spokesman said his death was not being treated as a criminal investigation and there was no question of foul play. Later coroner's officers attended the scene.'

That was too much. I left the office and walked briskly along the street, past the tower of the newspaper building to where the central police station squatted behind the Victorian red-brick law courts.

Nodding to the constable on the door, I entered the CID offices and pressed the bell on the counter. A clerk appeared from behind a frosted glass partition and, being told that I wanted to talk to Detective Chief Inspector Cyril McClellan, took my name and disappeared again. I looked around the room. The walls were covered in posters warning against everything from the colorado beetle to leaving your car unlocked. The solitary wooden bench didn't look inviting and I remained standing. From behind the counter and the partition came the sound of typewriters rattling.

The clerk returned and said that Cyril would see me in Mr Grey's room. I grinned. The gaffer was away and Cyril was using the facilities. Most of the senior detectives in Birmingham gave me the time of day, but Cyril McClellan gave me more. I had done him a few favours and we were as thick as thieves, in a manner of speaking.

He looked old and tired and the wide desk did little for him. I was flippant, 'Thinking about your pension again. Twenty years is long enough for anyone.'

Cyril was too tired for jokes. 'I'm pushed Max. What can I do for you?'

'No social call. I may have something for you, about this train murder. Understand you were looking for Leverton....'

Cyril perked up. He looked surprised. 'How the hell do you know? What the hell do you know?'

'He came to see me yesterday. Told me quite a story. I think you ought to know about it, that's all. I'll make a statement. Want me to talk or write it down?'

Cyril looked a little agitated. 'No jokes . . . not today. I've been on my feet twenty hours on this one, and now it looks nearly sewn up. Now don't make trouble, Max.'

'You know me better than that Cyril. If it were not important I would not have come.'

'OK, OK, you'd better tell me all about it. Talk my ears off if it makes you happy.'

'Well, tell me, are you convinced Leverton did him in?'

'For Chrissake, yes,' said Cyril, idly thumbing the local broadcast sheets which were clipped to a wooden board lying on the desk. 'It's the old story. Jealous lover. Both had the same tart tucked away in the country. Jealousy breeds hate. Seems he must have planned it to the last detail. Then he gets the death wish and finishes the job. Neat. Open and shut, eh?'

I didn't speak because a buzzer sounded. The speaker was on. A voice said, 'Sgt Thom calling from Dukeswood, sir. . . .'

Cyril grabbed the telephone receiver on the side of the set, and flipped a switch cutting out the speaker. I looked at the ceiling, then the row of portraits of past CID chiefs on the wall and a big map of the city cut up into police divisions with deployment figures. Cyril kept muttering affirmatives into the mouthpiece. Then he put down the phone and swung back to face me.

'That was the crime car crew I sent over to Dukeswood to help the local men go through Leverton's house. He blew the top of his head off with an army revolver. Pulled the trigger with the muzzle in the roof of his mouth. That looks like suicide to me. Firearms will carry out tests, but I'll bet it's the gun that killed Battersby. Jack says he left a note giving his reasons. The coroner's people have got that.

8

It was very clear. Now it's up to the inquest jury but that's how we will put it to them—murder-suicide.'

My eyebrows twitched. 'Did you check the handwriting?'

'Nope. It was typed on his own typewriter. I suppose you are going to tell me someone else killed him then typed the suicide note?'

I grinned with my teeth. 'I would not be so presumptuous.'

Cyril squashed his cigarette in the ashtray.

I knew he was not going to like it, but I told him just the same. 'Don't jump to too many conclusions yet. Let me tell you Leverton's story.'

Cyril sat silent while I echoed the words of the dead man. Then he pushed me over a sheaf of statement paper and dictated the official caution which told me that I wished to make a statement and that I would write it myself.

'The gun was still there then?' I returned to the facts.

'Yes, in his right hand. Was he left-handed?' I let the sarcasm pass.

'Did Leverton own a gun?'

'Not one with a licence. It looks like a war souvenir. He was in the Army and pistols like that are ten a penny. In the last firearms amnesty enough ironmongery was surrendered to fill a disused mine shaft.'

'What about these two men on the train—did you check at the station?'

'They were either figments of his imagination or he just saw two men and fitted them in to his alibi. Station staff at Dukeswood agree that only two men, descriptions fitting Leverton and Battersby, and five women, got on the train there.'

'Perhaps they were already on the train, waiting for him.'

Cyril was not impressed. 'Yeah, and perhaps they were hiding in his hat band. What are you trying to do? Shake our case or something?'

'Well, I don't know, the man came to me for help. He told me a wild story, and sounded as if he believed it. I just want to know why, that's all.'

'Hell. He had just killed someone and wanted a mug to help back up his story. If you had persuaded him to come in it might have meant a lot of hard graft. Could be better this way. He had not got a cat's chance on the evidence. It would just have cost the taxpayer money keeping him. There's nothing for you to worry about. You did the right thing.'

I got up. In that mood I would get no more from Cyril. 'Well anyway, I've set the record straight.'

He glanced up from the sheaf of yellow crime sheets he was studying. 'Thanks for dropping in. Complications are just what I need. You will have to be at the inquest. I will let you know.'

I had one hand on the door and the other resting on the well-thumbed legal text atop the bureaux beside the door.

'Right. We must have a couple of jars sometime. Like the old days.'

Cyril smiled a cracked and lopsided weary smile. I was half-way through the door when he called me back.

'One little piece of the jig-saw is missing though.' He was slouched back in the big chair looking at the ceiling. 'Battersby's housekeeper claims he had a document case with him when he left home. We haven't found it. It was not on the train. Of course he may have left it somewhere, or Leverton could have taken it. May mean nothing, but I thought you might be interested. He didn't drop it with you by any chance?'

I raised my hands and pointed to the statement. 'The truth, the whole truth and nothing but the truth.'

'Well,' he said, 'Give you something to think about besides those fat divorcees you're fleecing.' Cyril gave me a half-wave. 'So long, don't lose any sleep.'

'Cheers,' I replied and shut the door behind me.

I walked slowly back to my car, parked near the office, and I hardly noticed what a beautiful day was boiling up. The meter had almost expired and a warden was hovering. I got in, started the engine and pulled out into the traffic.

3

I drove back to my flat. I thought of Mrs Leverton, now living in Solihull and at last I picked up the telephone and dialled her number. She was surprised to hear from me, but I arranged to see her and within half an hour was driving to Solihull.

The house was small, detached and unspectacular unlike the split-level mansion that the Levertons inhabited in Dukeswood in the days of their married bliss, if they ever had any married bliss.

When I rang the bell, the door was opened by a grey middle-aged woman wearing a defensive expression and a shapeless dress. She ushered me into a room where Mrs Leverton was sitting on a couch with her hands folded on her lap as she looked past the velvet curtains to the long, already green garden. A closed book lay on the coffee table nearby, but I didn't get time to look at the title because Mrs Leverton was standing up, a little flushed, touching my hand and waving me to a chair.

'Now Mr Daly, what can I do for you?'

She was wearing a plain woollen dress that fitted closely to her slender figure. It was not black but a deep monochrome grey. I had never before seen her when her dark hair wasn't scraped up and back, but now it was loose and coiled over her shoulders. She looked at me levelly out of hazel eyes but I noticed her mouth was slightly tense.

'Your former husband, Mrs Leverton, have the police told you how he came by his death? I mean have they indicated who was responsible?'

Her chin rose.

'They said it appeared he had shot himself. In fact they asked me if I knew he had a gun and a silencer. I said no, which is perfectly true. They also asked me a lot of other more personal questions about things you know all about, Mr Daly.'

'They mentioned the Battersby thing and said they believed the deaths were connected?'

'Yes.'

'Are they asking you to attend any inquests?'

'That won't be necessary apparently. William's brother is identifying the body. . . .'

She swallowed. It was the first sign of any faltering. Her eyelids dropped and rose again slowly and she went on.

'They're apparently satisfied with everything else.'

'Well, Mrs Leverton, the reason I came to see you is because I am very far from satisfied with everything else. I believe that things did not happen as the police say and it may be that Mr Leverton was killed by someone else.'

Then I plunged into an account of Leverton's visit to me, the way the police regarded the episode and my belief that he was telling something like the truth.

'To be honest, Mr Daly, I don't consider that my hus . . . my former husband was capable of killing Mr Battersby. He would probably have told himself he would, then spent the rest of his time making excuses to himself to explain his own inaction. And I doubt whether he would kill himself.'

So she was still bitter. . . .

'Forgive me,' I said, 'but I think that's just about right. Which means he was killed by someone else.'

'Well that's what you say Mr Daly, but presumably the police know what they're doing. I mean they would investigate if there were any doubt, I suppose. I really can't think they would be so negligent as you seem to suggest. . . . I don't pretend to understand all this. It's so completely sordid. Frankly I just want to forget the whole thing.'

'Mrs Leverton,' I said, 'the police aren't being negligent at all. The facts as they know them point in one direction. If I were in their position, my reaction would be the same. Certainly there are loose ends; in any human situation there are dozens of loose ends and the police don't think that they add up to a reasonable doubt in this case. But for me those loose ends make a sort of pattern. To the police, as to any reasonable person, I suppose the obvious conclusion here is the one they have drawn. Mr Leverton's explanation is technically feasible but common sense says it's outrageous. But I've had more personal contact than anyone else with this case. I've seen your husband in some of his more . . . intimate moments.'

She flinched. I went on.

'I saw him and made an estimation of him. And I saw him again when he came to my office. There are one or two other things. You didn't know he had a gun. That's odd. And after the death of Battersby, his briefcase was missing. Your husb . . . ex-husband would have no reason to take that.'

Now she looked very grave.

'What can I do about it, Mr Daly?'

'Well, I'm going to look into this and I'm sure you'll be interested in what comes out.'

She was angry. Not at me, but at what she considered an unjust fate that had smeared a mess of these proportions all over her life. I was the person sitting opposite her, however, and I was the obvious whipping boy.

'What are you doing Mr Daly? Touting for custom?'

'All right Mrs Leverton, my conscience is far from clear and we both know that. Your ex-husband came to see me and I did the sensible thing, but now he's dead. Ever since, I've been telling myself that it's nothing to do with me but that's one argument I'm not going to win. I know your husband was an adulterer, and I helped to expose him on your behalf. Perhaps that means you don't care about what happened to him. You do, however, have a son.'

That was dirty, and I knew it, but as I said, my conscience was troubling me. Or perhaps it was just my professional pride.

She whitened. She thought it was dirty too. Yet she took the point. Nigel Leverton was ten. Now he was at preparatory school and in his mother's custody, but he was old enough to know his father, soon to be officially regarded as a murderer and a suicide. That wouldn't be nice for Nigel at all.

'I'm sorry,' I said, 'I thought we both had some sort of interest in seeing this matter was fully cleared up to both our satisfactions, but I haven't been very discreet. I'll go.'

She didn't contradict my last remark.

'You're quite right, Mr Daly, I do have an interest. If you can find out anything, you might tell me.'

'Well, I'll work on it anyway, but a fully documented report is likely to take quite some time. And time's valuable.'

'All right. It entirely depends on what you discover, but I daresay if you could produce conclusive evidence of William's innocence, I'd be prepared to pay for it.'

I didn't try to salvage my image. We exchanged the usual courtesies and I left.

In my car again, driving quite automatically to the office, I was mulling a lot of ideas over in my head. Working on the theory that Leverton had died because he had seen too much, the only course of action I could take was to approach things via the Battersby murder.

So I went up to the police station personally and hung about. After ten minutes, I met a detective constable I knew. He was going home and didn't want to be bought a drink, but he knew what I wanted to know. Detective Inspector Javan had conducted the interviews with most of Battersby's professional colleagues.

Javan, a middle-aged man with a long, bony face, was in, but he wasn't talkative. I managed to get him alone in the CID office of the station, and I introduced myself although he already knew who I was. His set expression didn't change when I explained I was working for a private client and asked him about Battersby. He spoke without opening his mouth, which remained a lipless line in his grey face. He couldn't divulge anything and I should have known better than to ask, was his opening salvo. He made a few remarks about overpaid incompetent private detectives, which were obviously his idea of humour, and I began to think I was wasting my time. I told him I would come clean and said I was clearing up a few odds and ends for an insurance company. He didn't exactly talk my head off then but he mentioned that Battersby's immediate superior at the GCC chemical works was a fellow named Roy Thorpe-Winman. You could see Javan was sorry he had let that much slip and he stood up, saying that I would have to ask his superiors for further information. I thanked him and made to shake his hand but I could see he didn't mean to take his hands from the pockets of his baggy, lovat-green suit, so I mumbled further thanks and left.

It began to drizzle as I walked back to the office. Inside I hung up my coat and reached for *Who's Who*. Thorpe-Winman sounded that sort of name.

Roy was not mentioned. In fact there was no Thorpe-Winman in the body of the book at all. There was one, however, in the year's obituaries. Nathan Thorpe-Winman it seemed had been a big man in the chemicals business and in the early days had done a lot to establish GCC as the giant it now was. From the list of his honorary awards from august academic bodies, he must have been a near genius in the laboratory. Roy was obviously the son of a father.

There was no harm in a chat to see what he had to offer, I decided, and reached for my coat again. There was more driving to be done, as GCC's headquarters was in a large factory complex just outside the city to the north.

The plant was large and sprawled within a perimeter fence. I drove through the main entrance where a works' policeman waited in his little wooden office.

A concrete drive led up to the main office block which dominated the expanse of laboratories and workshops. A small group of men in white coats came out and hurried by in the rain. I reached for the glass door, but it opened automatically on an electronic eye. The receptionist looked amused. I stepped up to her. 'I would like to see Mr Thorpe-Winman.' She was about nineteen and continued to smile at me as if I was the funniest thing that had happened that day.

'Mr Thorpe-Winman,' I repeated. 'Is he in this morning?'

'Yes, who wants to see him?'

'It's all right, it's a personal matter. My name's Daly. He asked me to call. Where can I find him?'

She told me the number of Thorpe-Winman's office and was going to ring to tell him his friend had arrived, but I grinned disarmingly, 'Oh, don't bother, I'll just pop up and give the old boy a surprise.'

She looked boubtful, but I grinned and winked confidentially and headed quickly down the corridor.

I found the room and put my ear to the door. I could tell there was only one person inside, having had a lot of eavesdropping experience. I knocked once quickly, jerked the door open, and stepped into the room. Thorpe-Winman was drinking a generous tumbler of Scotch on the rocks.

He had gone decidedly white about the gills and had slopped his drink. 'Don't you knock? Who are you?'

I walked quickly across to his desk and put the business card I had taken from my wallet in front of him and smiled down at him. 'Sorry to intrude, I will only take up a few minutes of your time, and I think you may be able to help me.'

He looked down at the card which carried my name in a rolling scroll across the centre.

Thorpe-Winman kept his hand close to the telephone in front of him, but he looked more relaxed. Wariness was seeping into his florid face and he rubbed the back of his other hand over the moustache which helped to stiffen a loose mouth.

'I am making some inquiries about a man named Battersby who unfortunately cannot answer my questions himself because he is dead. I came here in the hope that his colleagues might be able to help me.'

Now his voice was quite controlled. 'You're some sort of

private detective are you? Well I don't have to tell you anything. You have no right to be here. I don't have to answer your questions. I have already told the police all I know about Mr Battersby.'

I leaned on the corner of his desk. 'Yes, Mr Thorpe-Winman, but my interest in this affair is a little different from that of the police. Mr Battersby left one or two loose ends which are causing concern to certain parties. I am trying to piece together his background and habits so that I can attempt to clear up a few minor matters, that's all.'

He exhaled against his moustache, curling his upper lip slightly. 'Well, I hardly knew the man. He just worked here in a consultative capacity. I'm an administrator. I made sure he had the equipment he needed and that his reports were typed. We weren't friends. I hardly knew him, so what can I tell you?'

'Did you know any of his personal habits? Was he a drinking man? I'm sure you would know that.'

'Well, no, I'm sure I don't know, though perhaps I did spot him once or twice in the Club Cabana.'

'The Club Cabana? He went there often?'

Thorpe-Winman looked as if he could have bitten his tongue out. 'Really! I don't know. I drop in there sometimes. It's a nice place. I only saw him once.'

'Well, thanks for your help, old man. Sorry to bother you.'

I left him still sitting behind the desk, with the rain pattering on the picture window behind him. The passage was clear.

As I headed down the dual carriageway into Birmingham, I went over the events in my mind. My guess was that Roy Thorpe-Winman was something of a black sheep who had slipped into the firm on his father's reputation.

The day was humid, but I had to use the car heater to de-mist the windscreen and it gave my stomach an empty, sick feeling that reminded me I hadn't eaten since breakfast although it was late afternoon. I found a parking space, made for Dino's and ordered a large steak, medium rare.

*

The inquest was held the next day. Both deaths were inquired into together, following the normal practice when the police are sure that the incidents which resulted in the deaths are related. The little coroner's court was full when I arrived. We all stood when the coroner entered in his black morning jacket and took the chair on the raised dais. The evidence was paraded before the jury in the hushed courtroom. Relatives gave evidence of identification of the bodies of the two men, and an eminent pathologist gave the cause of death in each case. Leverton's was straightforward. A bullet fired at close range had torn the top of his head off. In the pathologist's opinion, the gun had been fired inside the man's mouth. There were powder burns.

Battersby's demise was the work of the same weapon. A ballistics expert confirmed that.

Next the porter from New Street who had found Battersby's body gave evidence. He and the ticket collector both identified Leverton as the man who had left the compartment.

Carol Morden, blonde, pretty and twenty-two, looked rather drawn as she gave her evidence and her voice faltered as she read the oath. Tight-lipped, she told the jury that she had known both men well, and admitted after persistent questioning by the coroner that Battersby had supplanted Leverton in her affections after the divorce case. She said she had seen Leverton get violent occasionally and he was inclined to be a jealous man given to moods.

When it was my turn I told the jury about Leverton's visit to my office and what he had said. A few eyebrows were raised but the reaction was comparatively slight. The foreman, an undistinguished-looking character with a blotchy face, was taking his task very seriously. He asked a few irrelevant questions about Leverton's apparent state of mind.

With the evidence before them, the jury turned their attention to the coroner who began to explain the case, and go through the evidence witness by witness. It had become very stuffy in the room but no one seemed to notice.

'It seems obvious to me gentlemen,' he said, 'that Mr Leverton was prompted by jealousy to take the life of his rival for the affections of a young woman. Perhaps in a fit of remorse he took his own life. Perhaps it was fear. We shall never know. Put out of your minds certain considerations that do not concern you. This is not a court of morals.

'Now can you say that what Leverton told that private investigator indicated that the balance of his mind was disturbed, or was it merely an attempt at deception? If you think that Mr Leverton's mind was disturbed, then add that finding to your verdict.'

In the well of the court, the reporters were scribbling. This was headline stuff.

After a short retirement, the jury returned with the obvious verdicts. They decided that Leverton killed Battersby and then killed himself while the balance of his mind was disturbed.

That was all there was to it. Mrs Leverton was not in court. There was no reason why she should suffer the strain of listening to a recount of the messy business. Leverton's brother had done the identifying and the family solicitor was there.

I was standing in the witnesses' room wondering if it would be wise to slip across the road and have a word with Cyril when someone took hold of my arm. It was Grey and he was not pleased.

'I would just like a word with you Mr Daly. It won't take a minute. Why don't we go over to my office?'

I walked with him across the street and into the nearby police headquarters, thankful he was not still gripping my arm. That sort of thing can damage a man's reputation.

The office seemed decidedly chillier than when I had spoken to Cyril there. Grey could generate an atmosphere.

'One of my inspectors tells me you were asking questions about Battersby's friends, and it seems you were out at the chemicals works yesterday.'

I made a mental note to leave Javan alone in future. He was not my type of copper.

'What do you think you are playing at Mr Daly? You heard the verdicts just now. That puts an end to the whole business. I don't believe this story about working for an insurance firm. I don't know what you are trying to prove but you had better not go any further or you will find yourself in trouble.'

He paused to let me speak. 'I have a client with a vested interest Mr Grey. Naturally, I don't want to embarrass you or any other police officer but I have to do my best for my client. You can understand that.'

Grey, however, was in no mood for explanations.

'Keep away from it Mr Daly. Stay in your own line and don't meddle in police business. You can take that as a warning. You won't get another one. If you come to my notice again, I'll get you for something, if it's only not licensing your television.'

The interview at an end, I left the office smartly but I didn't leave the building. Instead I walked down a long corridor past several courtrooms where the magistrates were in session to the licensing justices office. A girl appeared when I pressed the bell on the counter and I asked to see the chief clerk. A short middle-aged man rose from his desk and came to the counter. He looked annoyed at being disturbed but I presented my credentials, said I was working for an insurance company and asked if he could check the files for the licensing of the Club Cabana. I had to wait but eventually he returned and said that the club had been licensed for drinking, dancing and gambling in the name of Lucas Tait.

'Sorry to have to trouble you over this, but it's just a little insurance wrangle. Do you know if there was any objection to the licensing of this club?'

The little man pursed his lips and looked away at the window.

'Wait a bit. I remember this case because the police didn't like the place opening although it satisfied the most stringent fire and health tests. There was no formal objection at the hearing though.'

'Well it probably doesn't concern the firm I'm working for directly, but do you know what the fuss was about?'

He hesitated for a moment then said, 'If I remember rightly the police suspected that this man Tait was receiving financial backing from some undesirable types.'

He nodded confidentially. My eyes widened. I looked suitably impressed.

'Why couldn't they object then?'

'Well, the chap they didn't like, an American he was, the name was Raggers, or something like that, wasn't actually on the committee list for the club. The police just suspected he was involved. All those who had their names on the formal application were like Mr Tait with perfectly clean records.'

'There's been no trouble since the club opened?'

'Not that I've heard. I'm told it's very well run. It has to be. The police couldn't block it, but if there was the slightest trouble they would close it up straight away, I'm sure.'

As I climbed into my car again I let out a long whistle that startled a passing housewife. Not Raggers, but Ragas—that was very interesting indeed. I'd read an exposé on one Paul Ragas in a Sunday paper and it didn't suprise me the police hadn't liked the Club Cabana. Ragas was an expatriate American from Detroit who came here after the 1961 Betting, Gaming and Lotteries Act made the British gambling scene the freest and one of the most lucrative in the world. So Lucas Tait was just a front man for a Ragas syndicate.

It was obviously time I did a little socializing. I went home early, took a bath and put on my pale grey suit and blue suede tie. I introduced my shoes to a little black polish and in my only outfit with any pretensions to suavity, I drove up the Club Cabana at about 10.30 p.m.

*

The club was a mile from the city centre on the main road to the west. There was a short drive from the road opening into a wide forecourt in front of a large early Victorian house. The frontage had been painted white and there were Doric pillars on either side of the big front door. Above this elegant portal was a neon sign with 'Club Cabana' in copperplate.

I knocked on the leaded door and it opened.

'Are you a member, sir?'

'No.'

'Well that will be one pound, sir, if you'd care to sign this book. Then you can go in, sir. Membership, sir, if you wish to join, is twenty guineas a year, sir.'

'Thanks.'

I signed the book.

A corridor stretched away from the porch, a deep, plum-coloured carpet covered the floor and the walls were plastered in ivory with gold trimmings. A little baroque, but there were worse places in Birmingham. Rooms opened off the corridors with the names of different games marked on them. Baccarat, Poker, Blackjack, Chemin de fer. I stuck my head into each room in turn. There was no bar in any of them but black-dressed hostesses hovered with trays.

The room at the end of the corridor was larger than the rest. There was a roulette table nearest to the door and a large bar to the right. There were slender white columns with Corinthian-style decoration in gilt and in the aisles behind the columns were tables where you could eat.

French windows at the end of the room opened on to a small ballroom with dance floor and bandstand. Several couples were dancing and I walked round the edge of the floor to an archway on the left of the little stage which the band occupied.

A party of five were sitting at a table close to the archway which led out into the bar. As I passed, I noticed a woman with sweeping dark hair sitting in the group. Her eyes met mine as I went by. She looked thoroughly bored.

Near the bar I saw who I was looking for—Thorpe-Winman. He came here now and again he said, but if this was the only place where he did his drinking, he came here a lot. His watery eyes looked more codlike than before and his rubicund complexion was if anything even more flushed.

I walked over and sat down next to him. He did not look pleased to see me. I glanced into his glass and called over the bar, 'Two whiskies . . . make one a double.'

'What are you doing here?'

I reached for the whiskies and thrust the double in front of him. As far as Thorpe-Winman was concerned, that was true eloquence.

'Well, as a matter of fact,' I said, 'I want to apologize to you Mr Thorpe-Winman. I realize I may have been somewhat rude yesterday. This is my way of saying sorry. You're lucky you don't know what it is to have employers breathing down your neck all the time.'

'Why are you here?' he repeated.

I drained my whisky, snapped my fingers over the bar and went on. 'Oh, everyone has to relax sometime.'

The barman approached.

'Two whiskies please, one double. Do you like water, Mr Thorpe-Winman?'

He was startled. 'Oh, just a dash.'

'And some water, please.'

The whiskies arrived. I splashed one and handed it to Thorpe-Winman, drowned the other and put it in front of myself.

'Your manners were quite intolerable,' he said.

The remnants of Thorpe-Winman's patrician manner were not impressive. For one thing he'd had too much to drink and was slurring his words slightly.

I relaxed into my chair and beamed at him. He drank his whisky and looked at me out of the corner of his eye.

I leaned towards him and muttered, 'To be quite honest, I'm not very good at holding a lot of this stuff.'

His eyebrows lifted in a superior expression. He was rapidly losing any fear he had of me. 'Fella can't hold his whisky, eh,' I could almost hear him thinking it. He dashed his Scotch off with a flourish. I called for another and followed suit.

Under the influence of the whiskies, Thorpe-Winman was beginning to mellow perceptibly. I told him I was going on holiday next month to . . . I cast around in my mind for somewhere suitable—Cornwall. Where was he going this year?

Thorpe-Winman accepted the invitation to play man of the world and began to talk about his plans to go to Sardinia.

I looked interested and meanwhile bought him two more Scotches. The chant of the croupier came through occasionally. The flow of the lushington's chatter slowed and he became reflective, looking into the crystal chandeliers and then into his glass.

'The holidays are a welcome break for me,' I said, 'but for someone like you they don't matter so much. You have such an interesting job.'

He looked startled in a sleepy sort of way.

'How do you mean?'

'Well, co-ordinating all those scientists with that up-to-the-minute research. It must be fascinating.'

'Oh, well,' he said modestly, 'I don't understand half of what they do. I'm admin actually old boy.'

I grinned at him. 'Oh come now,' I said, 'perhaps you don't understand the intricacies but you must grasp the rudiments or you couldn't co-ordinate.'

'Well I suppose so.'

'Some of the research must be pretty advanced.'

'Oh it is, it is.'

'Will the loss of that fellow who was killed hold up research, or will you be able to keep things going without him?'

His face dropped slightly. You could see the alarm bells ringing quietly at the back of his mind. I hoped there was enough whisky in there to drown the noise.

'Oh can't talk about that sort of thing old boy. Not done, eh?'

I winked at him, 'Hush-hush, eh?'

'Rather.'

I bought another Scotch for him and this time had one myself.

'Let me do this one old boy,' he said. Obviously I was no longer quite at the bottom of Thorpe-Winman's social scale.

I asked him if he worked at home.

'No no, old boy, when I leave the office, I've done enough.'

'I bet. Still some of those tame boffins of yours do, I expect they can't leave it alone.'

'That's true.'

'Huh, that dead fella'—I dare not mention Battersby by name—'bet he did his experiments at home, even.'

I could see the bells going again, but much fainter this time.

'Well, not exactly.'

'He always worked at the lab, eh? Oh I thought you said he worked at home.'

'Oh no, old boy, he did his experiments at the lab and typed the damn things out at home. Formulae and all that guff, I didn't understand it.'

'Oh he noted results at the lab and typed and formulated them at home?'

'That's it old boy. What'll you have?'

I told him.

'What was he researching?'

That was too much even for the whisky-sodden Thorpe-Winman.

'Eh, what are all these questions for? Are you trying to get something out of me?'

His voice rose and I saw a couple of swarthy looking characters, who had been flitting about in dinner suits, exchange glances and gravitate nearer.

'Sorry, no offence. Please forget it.'

He muttered and mumbled incoherently.

'I must go,' I said. 'Can I give you a lift?'

'No thanks, car outside,' he said.

In the hall booth I telephoned an all-night taxi firm and told them to collect Thorpe-Winman and gave them his address. He wasn't fit to drive whatever he said.

4

Morning came dull and overcast. I looked out of the bedroom window at scudding grey skies and wind-whipped trees. Two cups of black coffee later, I drove to the office and there discovered my hospitality was getting famous. I had another visitor. He was leaning against the wall in the corridor and when I unlocked my door, he stood up and introduced himself as Mr Smith.

I led him into my room, sat behind my desk and motioned him to a chair. He wore a brown raincoat and carried a black-brown hat in his hand. His hair was black and wavy and his beard blue. He looked at me out of big, liquid, brown eyes. Mr Smith was definitely of Mediterranean or Near East stock, areas notably deficient in Smiths.

'What can I do for you, Mr Smith?'

The grin was big and slow revealing great white gravestones of teeth. The voice that followed was also big and slow with a slightly foreign accent. There was an occasional American inflexion.

'I've come about a friend of mine. I'm worried about him. His name's Mr Roy Thorpe-Winman.'

I said nothing, just raised my eyebrows slowly. Mr Smith went on.

'You see he's hitting the bottle a bit lately. I think he'll lose his job if he keeps on the way he's going.'

A pause.

'As a matter of fact he's having hallucinations I think and saying all kinds of wild things.'

'Well, what's that got to do with me? You know my line, where do I come in?'

'Well now. I want to help my friend Roy. I know he's been talking to you. Perhaps he told you what's on his mind. If only his friends could find out we might break him of this terrible drinking habit.'

I looked puzzled.

'Really? I didn't know Thorpe-Winman was in such a state. I thought he just liked the stuff.'

'Ha ha.' Mr Smith laughed lazily.

I looked more puzzled than before.

'Sorry to have bothered you if you can't help. Maybe I'm just clutching at straws. I'll do anything, anything to help poor old Roy. I just thought he might have talked to you, told you what was eating him. Maybe he told you some of his fantasies. Such terrible fantasies he seems to get these days. Poor Roy needs his friends.'

'The only time I ever spoke to Thorpe-Winman was at the Club Cabana,' I said. 'We just talked about his holiday in Sardinia.'

'You go to the club often?'

'No, I only recently found out about it. How did you know I knew Mr Thorpe-Winman, Mr Smith?'

Again the slow grin.

'Oh a fella I know saw Roy talking to you a lot. This fella knows I want to help Roy and told me about you.'

I could not have looked more puzzled. My face almost split with the effort.

'Well, I just wish I could help. You know he seemed all right to me.' I chuckled. 'Bit tipsy of course, but quite *compos mentis*. Seemed to be looking forward to Sardinia.'

Smith's eyes narrowed.

'Roy didn't get upset at all when you were talking to him then?'

'N.... Well, he did now I think about it. He was pretty drunk by that time. I was asking how much his holiday would cost him and he got quite stroppy. Thought the question was bad form, I suppose.'

Mr Smith was throwing his hat from hand to hand.

'Poor old Roy.'

He shot me a sudden, sharp look.

'It doesn't look as if you can help.'

I smiled. 'Afraid it doesn't.'

Mr Smith got up with his head on one side and looked at me steadily. He turned and opened the door.

'I won't trouble you no more then.' He glanced around the office and said, 'I'll find the door.'

It had been a bit elaborately casual but a pretty good performance. Still I was surprised he'd been sent. However good the performance, it can't hide a clumsy move like that. Who'd have though Ragas would be such a ham?

I swung my feet on to the desk and tried to puzzle it out. Battersby had been killed and it seemed his briefcase was taken. Whatever else was in the missing briefcase, it was likely to contain the results of Battersby's researches.

Someone was anxious about my conversations with Thorpe-Winman and they had thoughtfully sent Mr Smith around to tell me. Still thinking, I went out and bought another paper. A lorry carrying thousands of pounds' worth of Sluico washing-up liquid had been hi-jacked. Sluico was a product of the GCC group of chemicals. That could be coincidence or it could mean more. I had to get Thorpe-Winman. Alone. It was a question of waiting until evening when he returned from the office. I had no trouble finding his home address in the telephone directory and he obviously wasn't married.

I parked the car a little distance from the block of flats where Thorpe-Winman lived. If Mr Smith had been keen enough to come to my office then it was highly possible that he was having Thorpe-Winman's residence watched too. Leaving the car in a side road I walked towards the rear aspect of the flats. They were set in three blocks of four storeys with little balconies, and lawns dotted with a few trees spaced out the blocks. It was cool and blustery and no one was taking advantage of the greenery. A careful detour and I came up from a row of garages at the rear of one block and round the angle of a wall.

A fifteen hundredweight van with a florist's sign on the side was parked up the access road to the block where Thorpe-Winman lived. I moved carefully from the garages to approach the van from the rear. Inside I could make out three men, one wearing overalls in the driver's seat, and two dark figures in the back. They didn't look like florists and they obviously weren't beautiful people.

There was no way into the flats without their seeing me for it was early evening and still light. One or two people who lived in the flats were returning from work. I slipped back to the front of the flats where the drive opened into the main road and waited. Within a few minutes a smartly dressed young man with a bowler hat and rolled umbrella came walking along the road. He turned into the drive and was obviously making for Thorpe-Winman's block. In a few yards I was abreast of him on the opposite side to the florist's van, still partially masked by trees.

'Excuse me, sorry to trouble you, I'm looking for a Mr Thorpe-Winman and I understand he lives somewhere in this block. Can you help me?'

Bowler hat was very helpful. Yes he knew Mr Thorpe-Winman who lived on the third floor and he could show me with pleasure. I stayed on the blind side of bowler hat using him to mask me from the bruisers in the van and engaging him in animated conversation every yard of the way to the porch door of the flats.

We reached the door and waited for the lift together. When it came we entered and at the second floor bowler hat stepped off with a curt good-bye.

Thorpe-Winman let the bell ring a couple of times before he answered his door and then he only opened it a fraction. I took him off guard and fell against it with my shoulder, then stepped into the hall of the flat. I pushed him backwards, closed the door quickly behind me and slid the lock-catch home.

A quick glance showed my luck was in and he was alone. Thorpe-Winman was leaning against the wall, his mouth slack and his eyes cloudy. It seemed he had had a few already.

'Now Winman.' I grabbed him by the neck of his jacket

and jerked him upright. 'I want to know what Battersby found out. If you don't talk I'll break your neck. Whatever Ragas has got on you, it's nothing to what I'm going to do to you if you don't talk. You won't be able to crawl away.'

I threw him into a chair. I had to be very careful not to mark him and risk a bodily harm charge if he went to the law while scaring him badly enough to outshine Ragas and loosen his tongue. Thorpe-Winman looked as though he was going to throw up. He had gone a remarkable shade of green and I was afraid he was about to pass out. He closed his eyes and didn't speak.

I poked him in the chest with my forefinger. 'Don't mess with me, Winman,' I rasped, 'or I'll give you to the "punch-up" artists outside.'

I jerked him upright, heaved him across to the window and indicated the three men in the van. He got the message.

'They want you, Winman. If you're lucky, it's a few months in the major injuries ward. If not. . . .' I shrugged. '. . . Your next of kin will cash in on your insurance. Which is it going to be. Me or them?' I indicated the window with my thumb.

He spoke for the first time. Almost a whisper. 'No—no—no. I'll try and tell you what you want if you promise not to hand me over to those thugs. . . .'

He really thought the brawny trio outside were waiting for him instead of me, and that really terrified him.

'I—I owe them money. A lot of money. They said if I didn't pay, they would get rough. I think they would kill me. Lucas Tait is an evil man.'

Thorpe-Winman was whimpering incoherently. I whistled through my teeth. 'So that's the set up, eh? Tait's got the black on you over gambling debts. You're in the worst kind of trouble, Winman. Tangle with that mob and you'll end up reinforcing concrete. Listen, I'm the only chance you've got. If you try going to the coppers. . . .'

I drew my finger across my throat and nodded towards the window. 'They're rough boys from what I can see of them.'

He nodded his head.

'You got to help me . . . you got to help me. . . .' He was the second man I had seen that terrified.

Thorpe-Winman was slouched in the chair looking vacant. I remembered the load of Sluico which had been hi-jacked. I grabbed his tie just under the knot and spoke into his face. 'Battersby was working on Sluico, wasn't he... wasn't he?' I emphasized the question with a sharp tug.

'How did you know that? That's supposed to be secret. You're going to get me into a lot of trouble. . . .'

'Let's have it now. Winman, tell me what you know.'

He began to mumble, but after a couple more shakes, the story began to flow.

'Battersby was engaged on research into a side effect of the liquid soap called Sluico. There are huge storage vats at the works and he found that at certain temperatures, the liquid changed its structure—degenerated. We only talked about it once. He was excited about some discovery and joined me in a drink. He was bursting to tell someone.

'All he said was that initial tests on the decomposing liquid had revealed some sort of drug with addictive qualities, and he was continuing research into it. He didn't tell me any more.

'I had these gambling debts at the Cabana and Tait kept demanding payment. He threatened me with all sorts of horrible things. In desperation I told him about the drugs thing one night when I was pretty tight. After that they changed their attitude a bit. There were still threats, but they wanted me to pump Battersby about his work. I kept giving them phoney information that I had made up. After a while they found me out and began to get impatient. There were no more free drinks at the club, no more friendly chats. They started getting ugly. Said they wanted results . . . samples, formulae.

'I was at my wits' end and started drinking more heavily. Then there was the murder. I was terrified. I think they got tired of waiting.'

He looked pathetic sitting there. I could smell fear and whisky in the room—an unpleasant combination. But Thorpe-Winman's story made sense. It accounted for the killing and what had happened afterwards.

'You've got no troubles as long as you keep your trap shut. They've obviously finished with you now. I'm not going to do anything which will endanger you.'

Winman sat there shaking and I had to think about how to get out. If I just walked out the chances were that I would be tumbled and get my head broken open. I picked up the telephone and dialled 999. A switchboard girl answered and I asked for the police.

'My name is Thornton and I live in the Falcon Towers block of flats at Shelly Spire. I don't know if this is important, but I have been watching a van parked outside. It's been there most of the day and there are three men inside. It's got a florist's name on the side, but to be honest officer, they don't look like florist's gentlemen to me.'

A rather bored constable was taking the details at the other end of the line. Someone is always seeing something suspicious. I made the story a little more interesting.

'I would not have bothered you, but I thought it was my public duty. They have been hanging around for quite a time and when they put the safe in the back. . . .'

He stopped me then. 'Wait a minute sir. Could you repeat that.' His voice was quite excited. I complimented myself then said, 'Oh yes. It was quite a big safe. I have seen safes before. I'm sure I'm not mistaken. It's the duty of every citizen I think. . . .'

The policeman broke in to check my name and address again. I repeated the details.

'Stay where you are, sir. We will look into it. Someone will be round immediately.'

I put the phone down and looked across at Winman. Most of the conversation had gone over his head.

From the window I could see the men in the van.

A patrol car must have been in the area when the call was

broadcast. It swung into the access road and pulled across the front of the van. Three policemen jumped out and there was quite a performance going on. People dashed out of the flats to see what was happening.

It was pretty well dusk and in the confusion I slipped down the stairs, across the lawn, skirted the garages and then walked back to my car. Five minutes later, I had put a mile between myself and Shelly Spires. The thought of the expressions on the faces of the men in that van were something I was going to treasure for a long time. They were probably all CRO characters.

I considered going to the police with my new information, but decided against it. What did I have? A Sluico hi-jack and some chatter from a lushington, and that wouldn't make much impression. The best thing to do was to lie low for a couple of days. Then it would look as if I'd taken the hint and that would take the pressure off Thorpe-Winman.

I drove back to the flat. Before going to sleep, I thumbed idly through the month's copy of *Birmingham Life*. I don't really read that sort of glossy because I'm a social climber, but by looking at the dinner-party pictures, you could get an idea of who would be divorcing whom next.

The Chamber of Trade had taken a whole page to cover their annual dinner dance pictorially. Among the guests was the popular Miss Carol Morden. She was with a Mr Gregory Cooper, director of a successful electronics company. The caption described him as eligible, so there was nothing in that for me.

All next morning, I lounged around the flat and in the afternoon I went out to the bank. At the counter, I pushed a ten pound note towards the girl behind the grill and demanded four hundred sixpences. She looked slightly surprised.

'I'm a fruit-machine addict. Can't keep off them,' I said. She disappeared and I could hear her conferring with someone. They were probably checking on the note, noting the serial number and checking it against any lists they had and squinting at the water mark. That didn't worry me, the note was genuine. The girl returned and handed me four little paper bags of sixpences. I thanked her and left. Now I was looking for a gents' outfitters of the humbler variety. There was one in the district and I bought a pair of blue jeans, some canvas desert boots and a donkey jacket. Back at the flat I scissored off the bottom two inches of the jeans. I didn't stitch any hems up and if the bottoms frayed that was just what I wanted.

I ran a bath, stripped off and put on the jeans. Then I settled into the water and lay there until it got too chilly for comfort. Afterwards I had an uncomfortable hour standing in front of the gas fire while the jeans dried around my legs. When it was dark, still wearing the jeans, I went down to a piece of waste land nearby, taking the donkey jacket I had bought and an old frayed sports shirt. I spent some time rolling them in the dirt, marking them with stones and kicking around to scuff up the desert boots.

I put the entire outfit on next morning and began to walk into the city. When I reached the town centre, the air smelled sweet. It doesn't often smell as clean and fresh as it did that day. The rain had killed much of the redevelopment dust, and the army of workers who spend their time digging holes and erecting concrete monuments to the twentieth century had not had time to pollute the atmosphere again. The city smelled sweeter than I did. A little dirt, a growth of stubble, and the garb of a wanderer—jeans, open shirt and soiled donkey jacket—can change anyone's appearance. I walked slowly across the city centre, scattered the pigeons in St Philip's churchyard and then doubled back to the Bull Ring and into Manzoni Gardens. It was the right time of day for the beats to take the air. A few were lounging about on the grass in the churchyard and there were more in the little patch of greenery wedged in the cleft of the ring road which had been dedicated to a former city surveyor and engineer. I didn't stop, just strolled on, scuffing my boots and kicking the odd scrap of litter which drifted on the pavement.

I slouched here and there for an hour or so and then made my way to the city's art gallery. I walked up the steps ignoring the disgusted glances of the office crowd who were breaking for lunch. In the entrance hall I was stopped by an attendant. He stood in my path and I would have had to walk through him to get by.

'You can't come in here dressed like that. We have too much trouble with the likes of you lounging about. There's a law against you scruffs coming in here, so you can just turn round and get out. We don't want any trouble.' He spoke quietly, not wanting to disturb the art lovers. I mumbled something and left. Several pairs of eyes watched me walk back down the steps. The attendant stood at the door with his hands on his hips. A constable was coming up from the direction of the Council House and the bodies who owned the eyes melted away.

I turned into an alley next to the gallery where a wizened old man with no legs crayoned pictures on the pavement for pennies from passers-by. He started over again every time it rained. He had incredible patience.

I skirted the central streets which were getting crowded now and strolled down through the warehouse-lined back ways and across to Culvert Street. Half-way down was the Globe café, hang-out of down and outs. I pushed open the door with its cracked yellow paint and walked in. No one looked up. There were half a dozen people in the café, but then it was early for the regular clientele. A group of four youths in stained jackets, grubby jeans and straggly, shoulder-length hair were sitting round one oil-cloth-topped table. One of them was asleep on his folded arms. Another with a bushy beard was talking to the other two. They took no notice.

At another table a slim, sallow man wearing an old khaki parker decorated with CND badges flipped through a tatty magazine. He took no notice. I walked past them to a table in the murky rear part of the café near a bamboo partition and sat down. Two tables away a girl of not more than fifteen was sobbing silently, tears streaming down her face and soaking into the baggy, brown, polo-neck sweater she was wearing over stained white hipsters in the usual skin-tight tradition. I took no notice. Today I was a hard knock. I had been sitting there for a full ten minutes doing absolutely nothing and looking vacantly into space, listening to the girl catch her breath between sobs, when a hawk-faced man with the physique of a rifle pull-through left his perch behind the counter on the other side of the café and walked slowly across to my table.

'You want something?'

He made the question sound a mere formality. If I had ordered a gorilla sandwich I don't think he would have turned a hair.

'What's the cheapest something you've got?' I gave him a question back.

'Coffee tenpence, tea sixpence, you new around here?'

He talked in questions, with his painfully thin, bony body arched over the table as if he was going to skewer something with his hook-nose. 'I ain't seen you in here before.' Another question.

'Coffee—black. Nothing else,' I said to end the conversation. He shuffled over to the Italian coffee machine which dominated one corner of the place and started playing it like an organ.

The girl was still sobbing.

The group I had seen near the art gallery came in half an hour later as I was preparing to fend off the conversational advances of hook-nose. It wasn't obvious, but I knew they had seen me and I had aroused their interest. They clustered round a table at the far side of the place looking like an old painting of the last supper.

The girl was still sobbing. She had been doing that for ever as far as I could see. I spoke loud enough for everyone in the café to hear.

'Shut up for God's sake. You're getting on my nerves!'

Everyone was looking at me now. I was looking at the girl. Her face was like a big tear framed by lank hair. I let my voice blaze. It was a nice effect. 'Stop snivelling. You drive me mad.' I smashed my fist on to the table to stress the point. Hook-nose was at my side as if he were rocket assisted. 'No violence, mate. We don't want no trouble. You got a nasty temper. Leave the kid alone. She can't help it.' He had stopped the questions.

'Sorry Jack,' I said pretending to be working hard on controlling myself. 'I just get carried away sometimes. Bring me another coffee, eh?'

Everyone was talking again. The incident was over, but it had served its purpose. A few people would remember me.

'Name's Albert. All the lads call me Bert,' said hook-nose extending his hand as if he wanted to be friends.

I didn't move. 'OK Jack—just coffee.' My voice was back to normal. He shrugged away back to the coffee machine with a twisted half-smile on his cadaverous features. I drank the second cup more quickly than the first, then left. There was a lull in the hum of conversation as I stepped through the door and again I caught the almost imperceptible sound of the girl's sobs.

Aston is about three miles from the city centre. Among its attractions are a first division football ground and an all-night transport café. My interest was in the latter. I hung around the city until ten that night and then hiked to Aston. I had not eaten all day and my insides felt like a supermarket on a Wednesday afternoon. As always the café was warm and cheery with a few loungers about, a group of leather-jacketed rockers and a handful of beats tucked away in a corner. I sat by myself and ate sausage and chips with an enormous mug of tea. I stayed there all night, dozing fitfully. No one took any notice. You don't bother a loner in a shack like that.

Next day I went straight to the Globe where I ate a ghastly breakfast of greasy bacon sandwiches prepared by hook-nose who was pretending he was glad to see me. It was early and the place was deserted. Hook-nose could not stay open all night—the police wouldn't let him. I didn't blame them.

I told him I was sorry about the outburst the previous day and he seemed pleased I was sorry, but he kept on looking at me as though he feared I would go berserk and wreck the place if he said a wrong word. We chewed the fat for a while and were getting quite matey when the yesterday crowd arrived. I sat in a corner and read a copy of that day's newspaper which I had recovered from a waste bin. The disciples were talking about me.

In the afternoon I walked about a bit and strolled over to Cannon Hill Park and lay on the grass. For early spring it was quite warm. That night I went back to the café in Aston and repeated the procedure. I was dirty, tired, depressed and wondering if it was all worth it. I was wishing Leverton had been hit by a bus before he reached my office, or better still if he hadn't been born at all.

5

It was three o'clock in the afternoon when I went up to the fountain in Chamberlain Square. They were already there, sitting on the small wall which enclosed the pool of the fountain, half a dozen beatniks, the same group I had seen in the café. They were talking among themselves and I sat on the wall close to a hunch-shouldered youth wearing the dirty parker which is the uniform of the fraternity. On the arm was stencilled 'I hate work'. The back of the coat bore the legend 'Billy the Kid—hands off'. He had his back to me and was engaged in deep conversation with a lean, fuzzy-faced youth at his side.

I sat on the wall and watched the water. On the bottom were the odd bits of litter which adorn most fountains, a few coins, bits of paper and cigarette packets. I dug into my pocket and pulled out a fistful of sixpences, I could just hold them in one hand. There was no one about except the beats and I shook the little silver coins from one hand to another, then with thumb and forefinger flipped one into the fountain. It hit the water with a plop and sank to gleam on the silty bottom. The group stopped talking. They were just staring at me. I kept my head down as if lost in thought, shook the sixpences into a pile in each hand and jingled them. He was standing in front of me and could only have been the leader of the group, built like a wine tun, with a deep reddish beard and gleaming porcine eyes. His curly hair matched the face fungus and fell on to his shoulders. The group was silent.

'You flipped man?' he drawled with a smile on his lips. 'You must be a crazy man throwing bread about like that. Din' I see you in the Globe before?'

'Right,' I said looking up at his face. 'What's it to you?'

He was still smiling. 'Nothing man, nothing. Don't get excited. It's just that we don't see many wild men like you, making free and easy with the coinage of the realm. You an eccentric millionaire or something?' The others were clustered round me like a jury eyeing a courtroom exhibit. Only the beard was smiling. I talked to him.

'You mean these.' I shook the coins then dropped them back into my pocket.

'I done a gassy last night. So what.'

I tipped my head back and leaned on the wall with the palms of my hands and laughed lightly. They laughed too.

'Well ain't you the wildest,' said the beard. 'How come we ain't seen you about before. Up from the smoke?'

'Nope. I bin travelling the country a bit like. Thought I'd have another look at old Brum. I was legit when I was last here.'

We talked about nothing at all for a while, verbal fencing while they eyed me up. Then I said:

'I ain't eaten yet. The pie shop in New Street open?'

The jacket said it was and I scooped out a handful of sixpences and stuck them in his palm. 'Go and get some then,' I said.

He looked as if his eyes were going to drop out, then turned to the leader. The beard nodded. Jacket scurried away.

'That's kind of you, man,' said the beard. 'What they call you?' he asked.

'Teacher,' I replied, 'because I was thrown out of a training college down south when they found I was pinching stuff. I would have been a lousy teacher.' He laughed. 'OK Teacher. Thanks for the pies. We have trouble eating.'

'I just have trouble,' I said. 'The busies round here don't like tea-leaves. If I don't find somewhere to shack up pretty soon they're going to pinch me for sussing. I got my bit of form.'

The beard thought for a second. He said, 'You can kip with us. The law don't worry us, man, we keep moving and we got pads all over. You help us and we'll look after you, how about that?'

'Thanks,' I said, 'I'll give it a try, but the first rozzer to poke his nose in gets a bunch of fives. I ain't going back in the stir again. It drives me mad.'

He nodded as if he understood then added slyly, 'Anything else you want, we can help you, like the weed, man, or. . . .'

'Look,' I said, 'I ain't no junky, I don't need that clap. I ain't got strong feelings about it, just don't use it. If it's a screwing job though, I'm not fussy.'

We talked a bit longer, then jacket came back with the hot pies. We all ate silently. I didn't ask about the change.

Eventually the big man shoved himself off the fountain wall. 'Come on Teach,' he said, 'we're goin' down the Globe. 'Sgetting a bit cool here.' The others shuffled off in a little knot behind him.

'Ev'body calls me King, short for King Lear. That's because I do me bit of fancying.'

And he laughed at the pun.

'That bloke'—tall slender youth with big, brown eyes and black, lank hair surmounted by a blue Dylan cap—'that's Ned the Bed. And that'— a short, powerful-looking lad with a bad case of acne—'that's Spotso.' A girl in tight, faded-blue jeans with a man's zip fly padded behind Spotso utterly indifferent to everything. King didn't introduce her. I noticed everyone called the big fellow not King, but Red. Even beats will have their little joke.

Down at the Globe the beats collapsed into their seats. A couple of teenage girls were there in school uniform. Ned the Bed slid over and insinuated himself into the bench seat beside them. A moment's hushed conversation culminating in giggles and some shouted bantering and he returned playing with half a crown. Three cups of coffee were bought and everyone took turns to drink out of them.

The door swung open and a man came in. He was freakishly tall and thin. Six feet four and built like a hairpin. He wore the standard dirty anorak and some denim trousers. Perched perilously on his nose were a pair of rimless glasses. Behind him was another youth with curly hair and boggling eyes. His variation on the uniform was a tattered corduroy coat hanging somewhere between jacket and overcoat length. Both looked peaky and in need of a good immersion.

'Hiya Stringy,' shouted Ned. 'Christ he's brought Dragon with 'im.'

Stringy sat down, somehow managing to fold his length into the seat.

'Like hi, man. What's with you groovers?'

Stringy was a comedian.

Red slurped a mouthful of coffee and pointed me out. 'Meet Teach. Teach, this is Stringy. He's an intellectual.'

A few chuckles greeted that remark.

'That thing there is Dragon.'

Stringy fixed me with an inquiring look.

'Say Teach, do you believe in God?'

I laughed.

'Allah or Jehovah? Na . . . I just don't think about that clap. It bores me.'

Stringy said, 'But don't you think the Christian conception of God is sort of sub-anthropomorphic?'

'Very likely.'

'No, but if I'd made the world I wouldn't want people to walk into buildings and start singing Stringy is a flickin' good bloke and anyone who says different is gonna cop 'is lot. So I'm better than God see?'

'Yeah.'

Dragon sighed. 'That stuff hangs me up,' was his contribution.

'Shadup,' said Red. And he slowly produced a cigarette from his knapsack, lit it, and smoked reflectively.

Ned the Bed had seen another group by a table near the far wall of the café and he sauntered over to them. Spotso nodded towards them. 'Basket Ned's always trying his luck with the ravers.'

He noticed my incomprehension.

'They're part-timers. Not like us. Got a job, go to school just smoke pot on the side.'

'Yeah.'

Red took another cigarette and passed it to the indifferent girl. She grabbed it with the first positive-looking movement I'd seen her make, took the light and began to smoke.

'This stuff don' do no harm man,' said Red. 'I don't get hooked hard myself, but this stuff don' do no harm.'

'This is a good town for the junk?'

Red looked at me a little harder when I said that, licking the backs of his yellow teeth without answering.

'Yeah,' said Stringy. 'No sweat in this scene, man. Junk everywhere.'

'Mostly just ganja though?'

'Mostly yeah, man, but there's stacks of chemists to knock over, full of purple hearts and blue bombers.'

'Heroin?'

Red cut in, 'Thought you didn't junk man?'

'I had a friend. Down south that was. He took purples to get through his exams and bennies too. Then he got hooked on heroin. He din' bother with hemp or marijuana or none of that stuff. He just went from peps to hard. Soon he was main line. Should of seen him. He's in hospital now. Could be I'm chicken but it put me off.'

Red snorted, 'Clap. Pot's OK.'

Stringy had a logical mind. He ignored the intervention. 'There are hundreds of main-line groovers in this burgh. They get junk so easy, man, you wouldn't believe.'

'Expensive though. You blokes must spend a lot of moola on that stuff.'

Stringy laughed. 'None of us here now is main line. But no sweat if we were, man. There's about 80 registered addicts around here. They get heroin or cocaine from hospital, pretend they've lost it and go back for more. Docs always cough and they flog the surplus around. There's a bloke I know makes his own LSD. Some of the ravers are giving it a try. I'll settle for pot.'

'You get that from the spades?'

'Nah, they grow their own in greenhouses up Handsworth

or get it from Liverpool, but they keep it to themselves. We get ours from ravers or go hitching on the Continent and get it then. Morocco's a good place. Ever bin to Spain, man?'

'Yeah.'

'Hitch?'

'Yeah.'

'How you go?'

'Lousy. France is OK but in Spain I had to jump trains.'

'Same with me and Dragon. But once yer in Morocco cannabis is like spit in the street man. No trouble.'

'What about Customs?'

'Those baskets don' like us. So sometimes we slip the junk to some ravers—girls mostly who don' get searched. They take it through for us and we pick it up off 'em other end. But that's a bit dicey. If they get caught we're in dead lumber 'cause they can't keep their traps shut. Better if we can to rely on the professionals who bring it in pasted on the underneath of their cars with underseal. Jacks would never think of stripping off underseal looking for junk—neat eh?'

Ned the Bed came back. 'Wanna go a party?'

Red, his eyes bigger and redder than they'd been, looked up.

'Sure,' he said.

Details were exchanged and it was decided. We were going to a party.

We begged lifts to the party which was to be held in a large Victorian house in the Moseley area of the city. The beatniks turned up on scooters and in ramshackle cars held together by bits of string and the ingenuity of their student owners.

The party was in the top-floor flat of the house. A long landing stretched to a bathroom and off it a number of rooms opened. The walls were covered with garish cuttings from colour magazines, pictures of women, men and flans, puddings, landscapes, everything you see pictures of in colour supplements. We went into a room where the single electric light bulb had been painted red. In its livid light I could see the walls were decorated by dozens of signs stolen from the city's roads and conveniences—'Gentlemen please adjust your dress before leaving', 'Please deposit valuables behind the bar', and so on. The room was packed with young people who trod on each others' toes, milled about clutching at each other in sullen, arhythmic jigging, either alone or in pairs.

The next room we went into was somewhat similar. The atmosphere consisted of about one part air, two parts the sweet smell of pot and seven parts noise—the frenetic blare of an over-amplified rhythm and blues record. A third room I tried was dark and quiet. The only sound the grunts and moans of couples lying on the floor.

As I staggered back into the corridor I was confronted by a sweet-faced child of about seventeen. She was wearing a crocheted blouse and blue jeans. She lurched against me.

'You're big,' she hiccuped.

'I'm sorry,' I said. She put her hands under my jacket and ran them over my shirt. She drew a circle around a nipple and giggled. Then she grabbed me by the hand and towed me towards the darkened room. I resisted.

'I don't.'

Her eyes widened.

'I'm trying to find the dub.'

She giggled again and put her other hand into my groin.

'Sorry,' I said.

She looked a little puzzled. Then she shrugged and floated off towards the red room. I went back to the other room where the smell of marijuana was stronger now. Red was stretched out on the floor with a reefer cigarette. Stringy and Dragon looked pretty high too. They were talking to some people I hadn't seen before. These wore Indian-style coloured tunics and long hair decorated with flowers. It was hard to tell whether they were male or female. Billy the Kid and Ned the Bed were in the early stages of chatting up a couple of girls. Ned was justifying his nickname by the speed of his approach which consisted of grabbing first and asking questions later. I attached myself to Stringy's group He was squatting on his haunches while the others slumped against the wall.

'I mean, what sort of cat is this God anyway. I mean he supplies insufficient evidence of his existence and we all gotta use our free will. For some reason, if we decide he's there, that's moral and OK, but if we decide he ain't that's naughty and bad. Does that make sense? The only revenge we've got is to ignore him altogether. Him and the whole bit. None of it's worth getting involved with.'

At this the light of comprehension dawned in the glazed eyes of his companions.

'No, that's right. We don't get involved, we don't get bugged, we just keep cool and don't work or nothin' like that,' mumbled one.

That bit appealed to all of them. They nodded agreement. The conversation didn't do much for me and I made for the lavatory. It was just as big a mess in there as I expected. On the floor among other unsavoury debris was a broken hypodermic needle. Someone at the party was main line anyway.

I lurched back out into the murky corridor with its dirty yellow walls. Another bright young thing came swaying along, looked at me and announced that I was a disgrace to the party—no woman, no pot and no booze. I apologized. This girl was alive. She was wearing a trouser suit and carrying a plastic cup of flat unappealing rust-coloured liquid. She was probably the student hostess. She had Bohemian ideas but still looked sane.

'For God's sake have some beer, you're lowering the tone of the place.'

The grin came to my lips in spite of myself. I just couldn't resist it. She looked at me inquiringly. At that moment a big youth in a sloppy sweater spilled out of a doorway, shuffled up to us and pinched the girl's bottom.

'Come on, Jean.'

'Oh all right.'

She pretended to be annoyed with him, then giggled and turning to me, 'You can look after yourself? The booze is along there in the kitchen.' In the kitchen I up-ended all the canisters of beer. Each one was empty, affording a mere dribble of dregsy liquid. I decided I might as well get some sleep. Beatnik life wasn't agreeing with my constitution. Three days without a wash, and two nights' fitful dozing in a transport café with snatched sleep on the damp grass of a public park was the sort of 'getting away from it all' I didn't need.

There must have been some vestiges of bourgeois inhibition clinging to me somewhere, although they couldn't have been too noticeable, because I didn't select the darkened room to catch up with my shut-eye. The room where the beatniks were was too full of noise, so I went to the room with the red electric light bulb. There was music in there too—sounded like Jimmie Smith—but it was quiet and floor-centre shufflers wouldn't bother me if I could curl up behind a couch somewhere.

A couple of Jamaicans were leaning against the arm of a couch on which a couple pawed each other. The Jamaicans wore pork-pie hats almost without brims and they looked at the scene with complete impassivity. They didn't appear to be potted. They were probably just a status symbol for the party-thrower.

I threaded my way to the other end of the couch, found a piece of vacant floor and lay down. Strangely, although I was tired I wasn't able to doze off and I began to mull the whole situation over in my mind. And when I began to think I began to wonder what the hell I was doing. Even if Ragas was the villain and even if he was pushing drugs, what made me think he was pushing them in Birmingham, or what made me so sure the process he'd got hold of wouldn't take months to complete before the drugs started coming on to the market? Was I going to spend six or nine months living like this? I knew the answer to that question without asking myself.

As the evening wore on the place became more and more full. The room where I was stretched out became a heaving mass of humanity, some examples of which appeared to have brought that blood transfusion to all parties—more booze. When the door swung open for more people to lever themselves in, I could see the corridor was now also full.

I must have dozed off then and when I woke in the morning, the room was colder and emptier. It was about nine o'clock I suppose when I finally got up and stretched. The room was empty. Next door some of the beats were still out to the wide but Red was lying awake having his face stroked by the indifferent girl. Stringy was padding about looking through the window at the grey morning. Houses are never at their best after an all-night party. This one looked staler, dirtier, more empty-beer-bottled, fag-ended and fustier smelling than most. Our hostess entered the room in her workaday skirt and jumper, pulling at her hair with her hands.

'You'll have to go now I'm afraid. I'm sorry I can't offer you any breakfast.'

The beats, those who were conscious that is, grinned, said cheers, and began to collect themselves together, rolled out into the street and about a dozen of us began to walk back to the city centre. The world was already moving, humming, surging, with cars speeding by, queues waiting at bus stops, and labourers carrying things from vans into shops and carrying other things around road-side building sites. It was a world where you kept up your national insurance payments and got your card stamped, where you filled in details on the census form and worried about how you would meet your responsibilities to your family, or how you would keep up the hire purchase payments. It was a world to which our recent hostess was returning after a night in her Bohemian dreamland. And it was a world that had absolutely nothing to do with the twelve characters now shambling through the city's streets.

Forty minutes later we were sitting on benches in the gardens near the new shopping precinct. The conversation became hectic—Red spoke two consecutive sentences. His topic: food. Whether to obtain some, and if so from where. I could see it was time I justified my existence again. I wasn't a true beat, didn't contribute to their discussions about the philosophy of non-involvement, didn't smoke pot, didn't even lay pubescent girls at parties. I was the semi-beat crook. They gave me a cover and sex opportunities if I wanted them and I gave them the wherewithal to buy what little food they needed—presumably from the proceeds of crime, although they would be tactful about that and not ask too many questions.

I reached into my pocket, beckoned Billy the Kid and shook out a handful of tanners into his outstretched palms.

'Get some grub then. You baskets can do what you like but I'm bloody famished.'

Billy sloped off. The others looked at me without visible expression. I grinned languidly.

'I'll have to knock over another gassy soon at this rate.'

Red levered himself off a bench and called after Billy the Kid, 'Hold it kid, we'll come with you.'

Without a word, the group drifted in the direction of a nearby Hamburger Bar. The girl behind the counter looked doubtful as we staggered in and looked around as if for help. There was no sign of a manager to appeal to for a decision and when Billy dropped a handful of sixpences on the counter and asked for brunches all round she went for the food without a word. We sat by the window and an older woman appeared.

'I'm sorry we don't have what you want.'

'Right we'll have what you've got,' said Red.

She looked a little helpless.

'We don't want any trouble here.'

'We don't neither. We've got the money.'

She shrugged. 'Well, don't sit by the window. Sit over there in the corner.'

The beats looked to Red for a decision. He got up and sauntered slowly to the corner. The rest followed.

After the meal, which must have cost the place a few pounds in lost custom, the beats broke up. Red, Billy, Spotso and the bird began to walk towards the civic centre. Dragon, Stringy and the two who looked like hermaphrodites muttered among themselves. Then they announced they were going to a chemist's, and slid off.

I made a crude suggestion as to why the weird twosome were making for the chemists. Billy cackled.

'They're waiting for the heroin addicts. The registered ones who pick up the hard stuff. They'll get some off 'em and make straight for the nearest bog for the fix, or the nearest phone box or any old where.'

'Thought Stringy smoked pot.'

'Oh, 'im and Dragon are just goin' for the walk. Stringy 'll probably go up the reference library after. He's barmy.'

I noticed that Ned the Bed was no longer with us as we strolled through the city to Chamberlain Square but I forgot it altogether when we reached the Town Hall and found a large number of policemen about. They looked at us without visible enthusiasm but nothing was said until an inspector approached us as we neared the fountains. He asked if we were taking part in the demonstration. A crowd of young people was gathering in the square. Most of them looked like students and many carried banners with slogans complaining about the Government's policies in South East Asia. The students were gathered in bunches and a murmur of conversation, much of it conducted in north country accents, rose from each one. A fat man with unruly hair and rimless glasses buzzed between groups, ostensibly getting them organized.

Red licked his lips and grinned insolently at the police officer whose height he was.

'Sure man. We're in the demonstration.'

'Well keep in line and don't break away from the main crocodile or the fixed route. We don't want any bother to pedestrians or traffic hold-ups.'

Red didn't answer but he began to move towards the body of young people in the square which was swelling all the time. When we camped ourselves on its edges no one paid much attention although one or two of the more conventionally turned out students shot us looks of distaste. As the Council House clock struck the hour the student body began forming itself into a two-deep column and started walking through the streets. The beats tagged along. As Spotso said, why flip over what the crummy Government did? But it was something to do and anyway, as he said too, some of the students might be a soft touch.

After a leisurely walk through town which allowed plenty of time to look at the women, shout insults to unpleasant looking shop assistants looking on, and ask students for five bob in the name of fraternal fellow-feeling over the sufferings of South East Asians, most of the beats left the procession.

*

The rest of the day was dull, lounging in the square, sitting around talking to teenage girls and smoking pot in the Globe. At least that was the beatnik routine. I sat around looking as if I was trying to look tough and surly.

When the café closed at midnight we were thrown out. There were just the four of us together now—Red, Spotso, the girl and me. Red said it was time to kip in the derry. We started walking and I discovered the derry was the second of a row of empty houses in the Hockley area, just out of the city centre. The whole row was a red-brick hangover from the last century due to be demolished. Corrugated iron sheeting had been nailed up over the holes where doors and windows had been when these were houses and red and white signs said no one was allowed in the buildings which were dangerous.

We entered the first house through the back door where the metal sheeting was loose and movable. We crossed the bare rat-run boards inside and mounted the creaking staircase. A large hole had been knocked in the first-floor wall between that house and the next, and we walked through it. Now we were in what was once a bedroom in the second house. It was beat headquarters. Around the corners of the room were the rolls of makeshift bedding belonging to the itinerants. There were a few ancient haversacks. The smell was nauseating, consisting of a mixture of fusty rotting wood and mortar, pot and excreta. There were a couple of beats lying on the floor smoking reefers. In another corner a couple writhed in a sleeping bag. Obviously people were very sociable around there. I found a corner and curled up. Unlike many of the beats I didn't have a bedding roll, flea infested or otherwise, and I just made do by pulling my donkey jacket tightly about me and covering my feet with newspapers I had picked up. Until early in the morning there was the constant murmur of conversation between a few beats gathered in one corner of the room and the smell of pot was everywhere, but I dozed intermittently. I woke once to a swishing sound and saw one youth had moved the corrugated iron over the window near where I lay and was urinating through on to what was once the back yard of the house.

The next day was very quiet. We hung around and did nothing except wish farewell to Ned the Bed who had turned up to say he was leaving for Paris. All the beats had been there at one time or another. Ned said he was just dying to sit under a bridge over the Seine on a mild night with about two hundred members of the fraternity from all over Europe and sing folk-songs while someone stroked the chords from a guitar. He tried to persuade Spotso and the bird to come too. The bird said nothing as was her habit, but Spotso said he was waiting for the season when he would be off to bum around St Ives, looking for a love-in.

That night Spotso, the bird, Billy, another bloke I didn't

know and myself slept at the flat of a heroin addict in the city.

The next day was much the same. Red was temporarily off the scene and no one knew why, or if they did they weren't saying anything. It was after midnight when we crawled back to the derry and slumped down. Stringy and the Dragon were there. Stringy was as talkative as ever but the Dragon was asleep. The others didn't seem to mind Stringy but I definitely wasn't in the mood. In spite of their cadaverous features these beats seemed able to stay awake indefinitely. I lay down in the corner and tonight had little trouble in drifting from the damp rank-smelling darkness to the other darkness of sleep.

A high-pitched scream rent my slumber. Instinctively I sat up. From another wall of the room came a low whimpering, punctuated by the sound of choking. Otherwise the room was perfectly quiet. For a few seconds the whimpering went on, then erupted again in full-throated scream. A horrible spluttering noise, and the screaming became continuous, mostly howls but occasionally what seemed like a few half-formed human words. My eyes became used to the darkness but I sat transfixed although I could see that the noises came from a small bundle that jerked and convulsed against the wall.

Stringy's voice broke my stupor, 'It's Dragon.'

We reached him together. Dragon was bathed in sweat. I wrenched the metal from a window opening. The dim light eddying in from a street lamp seemed to drive Dragon again into a manic frenzy. His hands clenched Stringy's arm. His legs, rubbery, slithered and then thrashed the floor. His mouth was open but no sound came out except a strangled gasping and spluttering, and rivulets of saliva ran down his chin. His dilated eyes rolled but focused on nothing and his voice broke through again. Broken syllables, meaningless combinations of sounds, a wild, wordless delirium. I had the impression the other beats were awake and watching now but Stringy and I wrestled with Dragon alone. I threw my weight on his lower half to stop the obscene writhing of his legs. Stringy pushed hard against Dragon's shoulders and tried to talk to him. But the youth was beyond verbal contact. He began screaming again then stopped and threatened to choke on his saliva.

'Can't you shut him up?'

There was more fear than irritation in the voice of Billy from another corner.

I ripped a piece off my shirt and we turned Dragon on to his stomach to stop him from choking. I tied the material in a loose gag around his mouth. Stringy sat by him.

'We'll have to call for an ambulance,' I said.

'You mad, man?'

'No, but it looks as if Dragon is. I don't know what's wrong with him but I've never seen a fever like that before. He may die for all I know if we don't get him to a doctor.'

Dragon was quiet now. He writhed and twisted silently and hideously on the floor. Red must have come in while I slept. His deeper voice sounded suddenly from the darkness:

'Cool it, man. We can't call any doctor. They'd want to know who Dragon is and he wouldn't wanna tell 'em. Anyway this place the rozzers don' know about and as it's lousy with pot and half of these kids are under age, it's better they don' find out.'

'Forget that. If Dragon doesn't see a doctor he might die before morning. I don't know but he might.'

'Nah. He's shut it now. He'll be all right. We'll see in the morning. We can always call a doc from somewhere else then.'

'You stupid basket. It'll be worse if he kicks it here. You'll have a body on your hands then. I'm going to call a doc.'

The big figure of Red rose into the light from the window and he moved to bar my path to the hole in the wall.

'What do you say Stringy? Is he gonna die?'

Stringy looked up at his leader. Dragon had stopped writhing now and was moaning. I dropped to his side and felt his skin. It was still wet but quite cold. Stringy looked like someone being torn in half.

'I think perhaps he'll be all right for a bit. We can always see how it goes. P'raps Dragon wouldn't like calling in anything to do with the authorities.'

'That settles it then. He stays here till morning.'

'You stupid baskets. He's not thinking about authorities now. He's just bloody ill.'

'He stays here, right?'

Red looked around and from the gloom came a hesitant murmur of assent.

6

Argument was pointless and it was true that Dragon was quieter. I sank down beside his inert body. It was in fact getting quite late. Through the window I could see as I turned that pale streaks were beginning to striate the morning sky. Now that I was awake I was cold and I shivered. Dragon was shivering too. The kid was obviously very ill.

Red had slumped back again and most of the beats were making at least a show of lying down to sleep. The time seemed endless. Lying on my stomach I looked through the window hole and watched the pale streaks broaden and light gradually suffuse the sky. One hand strayed almost involuntarily to Dragon's cold and sweaty forehead. His eyes were wide apart but unfocusing and he was breathing through his mouth. I don't know how long we lay like that but Dragon began to shudder violently, his whole body heaving and his limbs twitching. It was too much for me. I jumped up.

'All right. That's enough. This kid's bloody ill and I'm gonna see he gets a doc. I don't want any stiff on my hands. I'm goin' now and if anyone gets in my way he gets bashed.'

The hard case act had its effect. Stringy looked at his friend and said, 'I think he's right Red, Dragon's real hung up.'

'OK, go ring for an amb'lance. We'll take Dragon to the traffic island down the road. Get the sick wagon to go there. No sense in asking the busies in here all the same.'

I knew there was a telephone kiosk a couple of hundred yards down the road, and I covered the distance at a trot. I made the call to 999 and said a vagrant was ill, very, very ill, and told the ambulance man the client was at the traffic island.

'I know you get a lot of calls, but this is truly serious, I think he may die.'

The ambulance man was polite and impassive and he said a vehicle would be along within twenty minutes. A handful of beats were carrying Dragon from the house when I returned. Red was walking a few paces behind.

'What you thinking of doin' when the wagon arrives Teach?'

'I'll go with Dragon. I expect Stringy'll want to come too. You blokes just fade when the ambulance gets here. We'll see you later.'

The beat leader looked at me quizzically as if he couldn't quite read a touchy tea-leaf with a Samaritan streak. I spat.

'I'm just goin' back into the derry for a coupla things I left there. Be back in a tick and see you at the island.'

He nodded and turned to watch as I trotted towards the houses. Inside I went to the haversack that Dragon used as a pillow. The room was empty. The beats had not taken their 'play it cool' approach to the extent of not following Dragon outside. I grabbed the bag and turned it out. There was a plastic mac and right underneath it a small pipe and a couple of twists of paper. I hurriedly unravelled one. Inside was a screw of brown substance—cannabis. I undid the other paper. That contained something else, a white powder. I sniffed. Quite odourless and amorphous rather than crystalline. A quick rummage through the rest of the bag produced nothing interesting, no hypodermic, syringe or dropper. I slipped the paper, tightly knotted again around the powder, into my pocket. The other things I replaced in the haversack which I dropped where I had found it. Then I ran back outside and up to the corner near the traffic island where the beats were waiting. When the white ambulance appeared down the road, the beats melted away with shouted good wishes leaving Stringy and myself to face officialdom.

The ambulance men asked if Dragon was the customer—an unnecessary inquiry in view of the sallow colour of his complexion and his now comatose condition. They loaded him on a stretcher and we clambered in behind as they slid it into the back of the ambulance. Stringy looked grim but didn't speak. The driver got in and we started at a slow pace. It wasn't long after dawn and there was little traffic but we didn't hurry. The second ambulance man sitting near Dragon in the back obviously could think of nothing to say to the two filthy wanderers sitting with him and the journey to the city's General Hospital was accomplished in silence. On arrival Dragon was slid again on to a wheeled trolley and rolled off to a cubicle where a couple of coloured doctors plunged in after him.

A nurse took us aside and asked Dragon's name. Stringy told her he was Terence St George—I still don't know if that was true—of no fixed address. She asked our names and we both gave fictional answers.

'No. No relatives that I know of.'

'Well, sit in there. I'll be along to see you with the doctor in a few minutes.'

She ushered us into a large waiting room. There was a reception office at one end of it not yet open. Apart from the door through which we entered there was one other way out —a large set of french windows opening on to a courtyard in the precincts of the hospital. The nurse turned and padded away. Soon she would return bringing a host of complications with her. I turned to Stringy.

'Right, I've done my bit. Dragon's got his best chance here and if it weren't for you baskets he'd have been here earlier. Now I'm off.'

'But. . . .'

'Look when she comes back there'll be all sorts of fuss and questions. We can't help Dragon any more and we can find out how he's going on some other time. Please yourself. I'm off.'

For the second time that morning Stringy assented. He shrugged and said OK. We stood up and I led the way to the french windows. They grated and squeaked a little as I opened them but no one came and we slipped out. From the courtyard we loped into a gully containing a drain between two block walls. It was a narrow one but we slunk along it and eventually got into the hospital drive. A brisk walk later we were in the wakening streets of the city.

'Right Stringy. Where did Dragon get his junk?'

'How do you mean?'

'Don't play games. We both know what happened. Dragon got hold of some duff junk or he took too much. Where did he get it from?'

'I'm not sure.'

'You must be. He knocks about with you. What's the matter? Did you enjoy what happened to him? You think it should happen again? Where did he get that junk?'

'Look Teach, it's no use causin' trouble, getting waxy. Cool it. You won't do anyone any good.'

'For God's sake, Stringy. Dragon could kick it in here without tryin'. I'm not going to smash anybody. Just tell me where he got the junk before I lose my temper.'

'In the Globe yesterday.'

'As usual?'

'Yes.'

'I thought he only smoked pot in that smelly pipe.'

'He did. I don't know what stuff he got yesterday. He got it in the Globe.'

'Right. Who from?'

'Dunno.'

'Strap me. Don't let's start that again you stupid basket. Who the hell does know if it isn't you?'

'Honest to God I don't know. Just at that time I wasn't there. He got it from one of three or four cats who push pot around the Globe. It could have been any one of them. I'd gone outside for a bit. Really I don't know. But he got it from the Globe. That's definite.'

Stringy was telling the truth. That was obvious.

'All right. Well I'm going down the Globe when it opens. There's no need for you to come. You can go back and tell Red about the hospital bit if you like.'

I could see Stringy was beginning to get agitated.

'Now don't get bugged. I'm not going to wreck the joint. I'll be really discreet. Only don't tell Red or anyone I've gone there. That'll do no good. I'll see you later. Don't worry about it."

Stringy gave a weak grin. I slapped his back and watched as he walked along the street through the crowds of manual workers changing buses on their way to work. When it got to white-collar commuting time I would visit the Globe.

There was a couple of hours to kill and I did too much thinking.

*

The whole incident made my skin creep. Memories of Dragon's wrenching screams followed me down Culvert Street. My nerve ends were ragged from the experience, and I was in no mood for the rancid, sweaty gloom of the Globe. For a few seconds I fought back a strong instinctive desire to get away from the whole nasty business and back to the world of people.

Inside the café a couple were necking in a dark corner, and at a table near the door a youth wearing grannie sunglasses and a stained, but still red, guardsman's tunic was looking at a copy of *The Geographical Magazine*. He was holding it upside down. Hook-nose was wiping down the counter with a grimy cloth. He had his back to me and I let the door close quietly, then tapped his shoulder. He jumped and whirled to face me. His face was ashen and his lips trembled.

'Christ . . . I thought you was the law. You scared the ticks off me. You want me to have a heart attack?' His whining voice was as dead as yesterday's news.

'Sorry friend. Didn't know you had the goolies.' I was standing close and I could see his hand trembling. The word had come down on the grapevine. I spoke quietly, 'Kid at the shack went screaming mad this morning. He was a mate of mine. I don't care two monkey's about the junk. . . . If kids get hooked that's their business, but this is something different. Somebody set him up with that stuff and I want to know who.'

'Don't drag me into this. I don't want to know. I just run a café, nice and peaceful. What goes on ain't my business, mate. These kids are wild nowadays. It's trouble all the time.' Hook-nose was scared sick. He was shaking all over now and looked as if he might fall apart.

'Who's the pusher, Jack?' I said menacingly. 'That's all I want to know. There's a score to settle.'

He looked around desperately as if he hoped the coffee machine would come to his aid. I spoke again. 'If you don't tell me then the busies will be down here like a ton of bricks. An anonymous phone call would do it. The kid's in hospital now and pretty soon people are going to start asking questions. I'm just the first. I know what goes on here and I could make it a rough ride for you if you don't come across with the name.'

I leaned on the damp counter and jerked my thumb at the interior of the café.

'Must have cost a bit this stuff. Would be a pity if it got all smashed up. The coppers wouldn't care. It would be doing them a good turn.'

I thought he was going to pass out. It would do me no good if hook-nose broke down now. I needed him to identify the link in the drug chain, the peddler. I tried a little sympathy.

'Look. I know you have got your troubles and I would not put you on the spot if there was any other way. I don't want to rub it in, Jack. I just want to get hold of the git who put my mate in the nut house. He comes in here doesn't he? This is one of the meets?'

Hook-nose nodded. He looked very unhappy. 'I can't stop them. It would be more than my life's worth. I can't. . . .'

I put my hand on his shoulder.

'No one will know you pointed him out. I will just sit in the corner and when he comes in give me the nod, OK? That way everyone's happy. I won't start anything in here.'

Hook-nose wheezed a sigh in agreement.

It was a long wait. I ate a sandwich and drank coffee while hook-nose fussed about behind the counter. The other three occupants of the café took no notice. The kid with a magazine had not moved a muscle, and a double bed was definitely the right place for what the couple had progressed to. By Globe standards it was a slow day. A few rays of sunlight began to filter through the grimy windows of the café as the afternoon sun cleared the warehouse wall on the opposite side of the street.

*

My dream of a plump chicken cooking slowly in red wine was shattered. A man in his mid-twenties, dressed in casual clothes: black, polo-necked sweater, dark-blue slacks, black, well-worn leather jacket and moccasins, had come into the Globe and was speaking to hook-nose. He was five feet eight or nine, and I judged about eleven stone. Unlike the beats he was clean shaven but wore his hair long. He was inclined to smile a lot as if his dental arrangement had won prizes. The smiler turned from the counter and eased himself silently to where the magazine reader was still sitting. It was the first time I had seen a glimmer of interest in the youth's eyes. He put down *The Geographical Magazine* which had almost become a permanent fixture in his hands and spoke quietly with the smiler who sat beside him. They were engrossed in conversation and I turned to look at hook-nose. He nodded once and then scuttled to the living quarters at the rear of the café. I sat and waited.

The two talked for a quarter of an hour. I didn't see the pass, but there must have been one. That was smiler's business and he could palm a fistful of dope with great expertise. The youth in the military garb pushed back his chair and left the café looking straight ahead. I glanced back to make sure the couple at the rear were still engrossed in the delights of the flesh. They were.

The smiler smoked a cigarette and took his time over a cup of black coffee. He barely glanced at me when I left the café. Outside, Culvert Street was bathed in dusty sunlight which made my eyes ache after the murk of the Globe. I walked quickly past the blank wall of a disused carpet store and ducked into the adjacent alley, narrow, cobbled and overshadowed by tall buildings. Down the alley was a row of overflowing dustbins at the rear of some small shops. I waited close to the entrance, gambling that the smiler would come this way when he left the Globe.

I heard the café door creak open and the scuff of the smiler's soft shoes told me he was walking my way. There was no one around. I braced myself in the alley and took a deep breath. As he came past the wall, I grabbed the left lapel of his leather jacket and swung him round into the shadows. Pushing off the wall I used the impetus to throw him against the brick face on the far side of the narrow passage. The smiler had stopped smiling and his face was contorted in shock. I grabbed his other lapel and jerked the coat around his elbows.

'Hello, scum. You heard about the Dragon? He was a mate of mine.'

He tried to kick my legs from under me. I stamped hard on one moccasined foot then brought my knee up into his stomach. From the way he squealed it might have been lower.

'Stick yourself,' he hissed through clenched teeth. I hit him in the face with my open palm, rattling his ivories.

'I've got plenty of time, pimp. It's going to be a pleasure working you over. You're going to have to crawl away like the filthy scum you are.'

He tried to claw my face, but I held his jacket down and his arms swung uselessly. I hacked his shin with my boot and threw him into a dustbin. The smiler rolled on the cobbles and I grabbed him by the scruff of the neck and hauled him upright.

Blood was trickling from one corner of his mouth and his face was smeared with dirt. The smiler had had enough.

'I didn't know that would happen. I didn't want to put that stupid bastard in hospital. He kept pleading with me to get him some of the new stuff. I didn't want to touch it, honest. Don't hit me again. . . .'

He put his hand to his face and I stepped back. I was learning fast, but that was a grave mistake.

Suddenly the smiler lunged from where he was crouching by the wall. I caught the glint of a blade as he swung at my groin. But the fight was knocked out of him. His feet slipped and he sprawled across the alley, the knife gashing air. I trod on his wrist then kicked the weapon away, snapping off the blade.

'Any more stunts and I put the boot in. That's a promise,' I snarled, kneeling on his back.

The young pusher was shaking from rage and pain.

'Spit it out. What's the new stuff you gave Dragon? Where did you get it. Tell me or I'll break your arm.'

To emphasize the point I wrenched the bruised wrist behind his back. It caused him considerable pain.

'The stupid kid. I told him not to touch it. I told him to stick to the weed or pop some tea for his kicks, but he begged me to get some for him.'

'Some what?' I gave his arm another playful tug.

'My contact, I don't know his name. I'm only a link-man. We don't use names. He gave me the powder and told me to lay it on the kids and see what the effect was. He told me to keep it for the regulars and keep the price low. Christ, I don't know what it is. He told me it was something new they wanted to try, promised me rich pickings if I did a good job. I didn't want to hurt anyone. If they don't get the stuff from me, they get it somewhere else.'

He was gasping for breath, and I eased my weight off his lungs.

'Who is this character, scum. Where's your meet?'

'He comes to my place, Friday nights and gives me a week's supply. I met him in a café. I don't know him and I don't ask questions. Let go my arm, you're killing me.'

'One more question, scum. Where's your place?'

'Flat on the Pershore Road a few houses down from Monkton Road. It's my bird's place. I kip with her. I told you all I know. Now will you let me go?'

He could have been scared enough to tell the truth, or else he was pitching me a tale so that I would let him go. Either way I had got about all there was from the smiler.

I dragged him to his feet. 'If I were a good citizen I should hand you over to the law for what you did to Dragon, but I settle things my way, punk. If you go to the coppers about this . . .' I waved my free hand round the alley, 'I'll make sure they get you for peddling at least.'

'I don't want no trouble . . .' he mumbled. I pushed him back on to the dustbin. The polo-neck sweater was grimy and his leather jacket torn from rolling on the floor. One of his trouser legs was slit from the knee down and he only had one shoe. He looked a mess, and I walked to the mouth of the alley and then turned to look at him. He had not moved. Then I slipped quickly down Culvert Street and weaved through the back streets in the direction of Hockley. I must have looked pretty dishevelled myself and I didn't want to arouse any suspicious policemen. The pubs were open and I made for one frequented by labourers from the building sites. In the gents I got the worst of the grime off my face with an equally grimy towel and dusted down my clothes. Then I treated myself to a quick beer in the bar to wash the taste out of my mouth. No one took any notice.

*

Billy the Kid was alone at the derelict house.

'Hi, Teach,' he said when I walked into the bare room. 'Where you bin. We thought you split the scene without giving us the word.' He was lounging on a grubby sheepskin coat which he had stolen from a hotel while the cloakroom attendant was away. The Kid was very proud of his coat.

'I bin casing this place on the other side of town. Might knock it over some time, but you got to be careful. Needs lots of preparation. Only the amateurs do a job without the planning and they get caught. Makes you spit. Screwing is a craft you have to learn slow.'

The Kid looked impressed and I dropped to the floor beside him. 'How's Dragon?' I said.

'Dragon! He was flying so high he was in orbit man. They won't ever get him down.'

I asked where the others were and he said they had gone over to a rough cider party in the grounds of some big house in Wythall as uninvited guests. He said he didn't feel like a party and had decided to meditate a little. I thought he felt badly about Dragon but I didn't say anything.

'Looked in the Globe earlier,' I offered to spark off the conversation.

He nodded, then I said as casually as I could, 'Some creep in there who kept on smiling, looked like he was pushing. I hadn't seen him before.'

'Got to be Sailor,' said the Kid without interest. 'He used to be one of us until he took a regular job—pushing dope.' He creased himself laughing.

'Why call him Sailor?' I asked.

'He was always yapping about how good it must have been to cruise the ocean under the stars. He was a real twit. Then he took up pushing and we gave him the breeze. Mostly he sticks to the young kids. He wouldn't try anything over on us. We got our own supply.'

I thought about Dragon. The Kid didn't know everything, but I let it pass.

'He sleep around too?' I asked. 'Looks too well dressed for sleeping rough.'

The Kid was warming to the topic. 'Nah. Ever since he started getting wages he got himself a shack down Memorial Row, living with some brass. What you want to know for?'

'Just interested,' I replied. 'He got on my nerves. Smiles too much. It would be dead easy to do his drum, Kid. Man in his line of business isn't going to squeal to the busies, and there might be a few quid in there.'

The Kid nodded. 'Yeah, why not. It would serve the creep right. Sort of instant justice.' He killed himself laughing.

'It's a great idea. We can walk around there and I'll

point the place out to you for a share of the loot. Why should a twit like the Sailor have it easy anyway? We'll teach him a lesson.' He laughed so much I thought he would injure himself.

So the smiler had at least one gift—he could lie convincingly in the tightest pinch. It was what I had expected.

I matched Billy the Kid's long ambling gait across the city. It was dark and once we had left behind the neon and mercury vapour of the central complex only the occasional street lamp dropped a pool of light in the darkness.

Memorial Row didn't boast the most desirable residences in the city. It was earmarked for redevelopment and already some of the back to back terraces of poky little one-up, one-down houses had been pulled down. We came to an open space flanked by hoardings with peeling advertisement posters, and the young beat gripped my arm then drew me across some adjoining rubble. When we were concealed behind a partly demolished wall, he spoke for the first time.

'Over there Teach.' He extended his arm and pointed to the grim block of dwellings on the far side of the road.

'Two down from the entry. Real high society.' His acne-pitted face broke in a grin. 'Fancy screwing it now? You could teach me some tricks.'

I damped his enthusiasm. 'Christ no. The boozers ain't shut yet. We'd get pinched for sure. Now I got a fix on the place I got to do some obo first. Get the lie of the land and the local habits. Then I promise you it will crack sweet as a nut.'

The Kid saw the logic in that and agreed there was no sense in being hasty. I memorized the details of the area then tapped him on the shoulder.

'I seen enough for tonight. Let me do this my way. You'll get your share. When I'm working I like to be alone. It's always been my MO, but I don't ever welsh on a mate. You can trust me.'

He nodded, and we strolled back to the sleeping accommodation the council had unwittingly provided for us.

7

For the first two evenings my vigil was unrewarded. Occasionally an unsavoury-looking character would call at the house, but there was no one who looked remotely like a supplier. The beats accepted my night-time activities and asked no questions. In fact they were eager to help. I told Red I would be able to expand my criminal enterprise if I could move more easily, and the beatnik leader introduced me to a student who lent me an aged motor scooter.

On the third night I climbed to the roof of a derelict shop next to the tumble-down wall where Billy the Kid had first pointed out the Sailor's drum. The spot was an ideal vantage point for keeping watch on the house as the only access was a door which opened directly on to the street and from where I lay, fifteen feet above the ground, invisible to passers-by and the occasional policeman, I had a perfect view of the house front.

It must have been close to midnight when things began happening. During the early part of the evening there were a few callers at the house and in every case the woman, who I supposed was the prostitute Billy had mentioned, answered the door. I thought it would be amusing at some future time to tip the vice squad about her activities and I was building up quite a vivid picture of what was probably happening inside the little hovel when events took a turn for the better.

There was nothing particularly unusual about the car. It was a rather well-preserved Mark II Zephyr, but the man who got out after parking close to Sailor's front door was smartly dressed in a dark suit and wearing a hat. Even more interesting he was carrying a small hand case, and this time Sailor himself ushered the visitor inside.

I scrambled down from the roof by the rickety stairs that led up to the skylight and slipped around the corner to where I had parked the scooter. There was no possible way of confirming that the man in the house was the supplier but that was a gamble I would have to take. If he turned out to be Sailor's cousin on a visit from Tilbury, I would be back on the roof tomorrow night. The old scooter started first time and I moved around the corner into Memorial Row and let the machine idle at the kerbside while I fiddled with the handlebar mirror.

The caller left the house after only a few minutes, glanced up and down the street, then got into the car and drove towards the traffic lights at Hagley Road. I followed at a reasonable distance. The Zephyr stopped in the centre lane at the lights, intending to travel straight on, so I passed on the inside, turned left on the filter light, then right up the first side street which brought me out ahead of the Zephyr on the main road. In the mirror I saw the lights change and I kept on going. We were on the ring road and I could tail him from in front. There was nowhere else to go but straight on.

The Zephyr moved off and I kept him a good distance behind. His lights were easily recognizable and traffic was light. Five minutes steady driving and I approached a large roundabout. In the mirror I saw the car was signalling a left turn. I went all the way round the island and followed, well to the rear. This was a tricky bit, because there was little traffic on the minor roads and I didn't dare to go too close. We entered a tree-lined avenue of decayed mansions, in multi-occupation. The Zephyr left-turned into a similar street of Victoriana. I stopped at the corner and saw the car swing into the drive of a house half-way down. Cutting the engine I left the scooter leaning against the gutter, and slipped down the road under the cover of the trees. The time switch extinguished the street lights to give me extra blackness and I took a careful look at the house. The big car filled the drive, and the crumbling house rose like a black cliff behind it. There was no gate, and screwed to a lone post protruding from an overgrown hedge was an ornate name plate which was the last link with more elegant times. 'Tarrasch' said the sign.

I walked away from the house keeping close to the hedge. The scooter took me back to the derry and the beatniks.

Being a large Victorian house Tarrasch had plenty of sash windows. I canvassed the beats for the tools I would need, a torch and a knife with a long, thin but sturdy blade. The knife was no problem. They all carried them to cut cannabis and one fitted the bill. I told its owner I was borrowing it and would repay the favour by crossing his palm in silver tanners. A similar offer failed to produce a torch immediately. The beats weren't affluent enough to own one.

Billy the Kid thought about it for a while, then said he knew who had one. I told him I had a job to do that required it. He grinned and left. I lay down and dozed fitfully. In an hour Billy was back with a torch.

'Give it back when you've finished,' he said.

I grunted assent and didn't ask any questions.

For another hour I dozed, then I got on the scooter again and headed back to Tarrasch. I parked around the corner and loitered. The streets were quite deserted at that time of the morning and I passed several minutes praying that an industrious bobby wouldn't come by and start asking embarrassing questions. Eventually, cold, stiff and tired, I approached the house.

Between the drive-top garage and the front of the house itself was a wooden door or gate that presumably led around to the back. It was locked but not difficult to climb using the handle as a hand and foothold. I swung off it and dropped lightly into an entry on the other side. The wall of the house was to my right, the garage to my left. There was another door at the other end of the passage and in front of it a dustbin. I moved the bin, which smelled unpleasant but contained nothing that rattled, until it was under a large sash window. If that window illuminated a room where the folks in the house kept a watchdog, I was in trouble.

I stood on the bin and leaned on the bottom half of the window. A tiny gap opened between the two panes and I took the knife from my pocket and slipped it into the crack. Manœuvring it until I made contact with the catch I began to press. Nothing gave. I withdrew the knife, reinserted it and tried pushing in the other direction. There was a small scraping sound and the catch slid back. Hoping the sash wasn't broken I crouched on the bin and began to slide the lower half of the window up. I jumped off the bin and rolled it back to its original resting place before returning to the window and pulling myself up on to the sill. Then I was inside the room.

It was dark inside. I slid the window closed and re-engaged the catch. My eyes were becoming used to the darkness and I saw I was in some sort of breakfast room. The floor was tiled and there was a table in the middle of the room. A door to the left, tentatively opened, revealed a scullery with sink, gas cooker and refrigerator. There was another door to the right and I quietly turned the handle. The door creaked and opened on to a passageway.

The whole house was as quiet as you would expect at three o'clock in the morning. A clock somewhere chimed the hour. A doorless cloakroom lay to the right and ahead the carpeted passageway opened into a hallway. I almost missed the little door to my left. A series of holes which I felt in its panelling revealed it provided access to a pantry. Every footstep seemed to cause a creak or a groan from the floor and I stopped and listened to the silence. What I was looking for would probably be in either an attic or a cellar. The attic would be on the second floor up two flights of creaking stairs past rooms which presumably contained the sleeping inhabitants of the house. The cellar. Where would that be? In a house like this you would probably get to it via a door under the stairs or possibly through the pantry.

I turned and tiptoed back to the pantry door, reached for the knob, found it after some groping and turned it. I kneeled down and after feeling for milk bottles or other noisy obstacles, I stepped inside. I closed the door behind me with a click and switched the torch on. Its yellow beam revealed that the pantry was almost empty and ended in another plain wooden door. This was locked. The lock was of the old mortise type but I couldn't pick it. It would have to be done the long way. I took the knife out, and using the blade began to unscrew the catch retainer from the door frame. Eventually the piece of metal came away in my hand. The lock was still fast but now it didn't fit into anything on the jamb and the door opened. Complete blackness lay beyond. The faltering light of the torch lit a flight of stone stairs going down. Twenty hesitant steps later I was in the dank cellar. A solitary chink of light in one corner showed where the coal chute and ground-level grating were. There was no coal there now. Instead a large metal tank supported by a tripod held the middle of the floor. A pipe emerged from it and ran to a miniature tower-like structure about three feet high. I flashed my torch and in a corner saw a number of canisters. I took one. It was sealed but I opened it with my knife. It contained an odourless white powder. In another corner was a mound of empty Sluico bottles of the squeezable plastic variety. Whatever the details, the tower was some sort of separator; the Sluico went into the tank and the white powder was one of the end products.

I went back to the Sluico bottles and took one that had about a quarter of an inch of liquid left in the bottom and stuffed it into my pocket. I poured some powder from the opened canister into my grimy handkerchief, which I knotted and rammed into a different pocket. I was standing in the middle of the cellar consciously memorizing as many details of the apparatus as I could when I heard the footfall on the last of the cellar steps.

I must have been too engrossed to hear the man inching down the stairs but I was suddenly aware of his presence. I quarter-turned until I had that dark area which was the opening to the stairs visible in the corner of my eye. Then

I stood still and did nothing. Still I couldn't make anything out in the gloom. He had covered the five yards between us and was almost on me before I realized he was finally coming. Then I hurled myself to one side almost overbalancing. The torch swung and in its beam I saw a large, black shape. He was big, my attacker, and he carried a length of something in his hand. No doubt it was something heavy. He was off balance after missing me with his lunge. I ran at him and smashed at his head with the torch. He parried with the object he was carrying and my wrist jarred painfully. He straightened. His free hand went for my throat. I caught it with an upward sweep of my hand. We grappled and instinctively my left knee came across to protect my groin. Sure enough, his knee came up almost immediately and slammed with a bony crack into my thigh. I kicked savagely at his shin. Once, twice. His weight came on to me. He was heavy. Too heavy.

We reeled against a wall that saved me going over backwards. I slid down as the pipe he was carrying clanged into the bricks over my head. There was the opening. I thrust the torch end-on like a dagger into his chest and stomach. The big man grunted and jack-knifed. The torch fell. I clasped my hands, dropped them on to the back of his neck and pulled his head further down as I brought my knee up with all the force I had. It smashed into his face snapping his head back. He groaned inert on the floor. I picked up the torch which was still shining and hit him again on the shoulder not far from the base of his neck.

Now he was quiet. I checked that he was still breathing. We must have made some noise. I had to get out. Momentarily I stopped and listened but the house was still quiet. This was a complication and somehow I had to allay the suspicions that would be aroused by a stranger prowling this cellar in the early hours of the morning. If the inhabitants got frightened they might shut up shop and Leverton would remain a murderer and suicide in the eyes of the law for ever. My eyes and torch ran around the cellar and in one corner they alighted on an answer—the gas meter. A broken gas meter emptied of its contents might explain the presence of a violent vagrant in the cellar. I broke open the cash drawer pretty quickly. It was the first time I had burgled a gas meter but I knew the theory. On the floor the big man was still asleep. I tipped the contents into my already bulging pockets and looked around again. Upstairs I fancied I heard someone move about. I picked up the opened powder canister and placed it under the chute. Standing on it I could just reach the grating to unslip the catch but as it opened upwards and outwards there was no way to lift it. I jumped down, went to the big man, and saw he had dropped the iron pipe he was carrying for my benefit. I took it and managed to push the grating open with that.

A voice echoed down the stairs:

'Mac. Is that you down there? What's up Mac?'

I dropped the pipe, gave a little jump off the canister and gripped the edges of the grating hole. As steps began to sound on the stone stairs I hauled myself out of the cellar, stood up and replaced the grating lid with a clang. I was at the rear of the house, on the path leading to the garden. A light on in an upstairs room showed there was a fence at the bottom of the garden across a lawn and some fallow flower beds. I ran for it. The fence was low, I was over in a moment and in an unmade pathway between the garden fences of houses and a row of prefabricated garages. I sprinted for the main road. Soon I was on the scooter and heading for the derry. I slipped into place in the room. No one appeared to be awake and there must have been some function on somewhere because there seemed to be fewer beats about than usual. It was already almost dawn. I should not sleep long.

8

When I woke the room was damp and chilly. Hunched in the corner, Red and Billy the Kid were playing dice on the floor. They were tossing the ivory cubes with expressions of studied boredom. In turn they were drinking from a bottle of milk probably stolen from a doorstep during a dawn foraging excursion. The loaf of bread lying on the floor beside the two had been acquired in a similarly resourceful way.

Red saw I was awake. 'Breakfast, Teach?' he said, handing me a hunk of bread.

The Kid proffered a second bottle of milk which had been concealed in his old army rucksack.

'Nicked,' he said sardonically. 'You ain't the only tea-leaf in town.'

Outside I could see the morning was overcast.

'Just the best,' I quipped back. 'That's why I got to fade. An itch tells me the coppers are getting my speed. I got to move on, else I'll get nicked and make big waves for you blokes. I'm heading south today. If the law comes round, you've never heard of me.'

I had a couple of pounds' worth of tanners left. Throughout the time I had been living with the beats I had kept the money in an inside pocket of my donkey jacket, and had slept with it underneath me to discourage pickpockets. There was no honour among thieves. Now I took the handful of coins out of the pocket and piled them on the floor between the two beatniks.

I spoke to Billy the Kid. 'That's your cut from the Sailor's joint. Nothing worth nicking so I done the gassy.'

Without speaking the two divided the sixpences equally and pocketed them, then Red said, 'Bin nice having you Teach. Any time you fancy coming back remember you got mates here.'

I put on the donkey jacket and walked to the improvised door. 'So long blokes.'

'Keep cool man,' they replied as I ducked through the hole.

The thought of a bath and some decent food filled my mind as I walked stiffly down the rickety stairs. What had once been the hall of the house was strewn with rubble and the downstairs rooms were dank, and uninhabitable even for the beats. Moisture ran down the moss-streaked walls, where remnants of old wallpaper were still clinging. There were no doors, they had been salvaged long ago by the local kids for firewood.

The man standing in front of me had materialized like a ghost. He must have been waiting in the doorway. It was the young pusher and he was smiling. We both knew why he was smiling. The small, black revolver in his hand was pointed at my stomach.

'I'm going to fill you full of holes, creep. No one muffs me and gets away with it.'

He stepped towards me, but the pistol didn't waver. I froze rigid. A certain nervous edge in the pusher's voice told me he was not joking. With the uneven footing, he would be able to get at least two shots off before I could jump him. One in the stomach and another in the head. I didn't move a muscle. The Sailor's eyes were wide and staring, and his clothes were rumpled as if he had slept in them. The smile was gone and his lower lip hung loose. He was steeling himself to pull the trigger.

He was close enough for me to recognize the revolver—an Italian-made Mondiall Brevitatta ·22 starting pistol intended to fire blank cartridges. It was favoured by tearaways, because the barrel and chambers were easily drilled out to take live ammunition.

I sought frantically for some diversion, but there was nothing. My voice sounded high and cracked:

'Don't be stupid. Shoot me and the coppers will hunt you down like an animal. Put that gun away, I'm leaving Brum. I won't bother you any more.'

I don't think he heard me.

'You duffed me up—I don't take it from no one. Now you're going to cop your lot. . . .'

The knuckle of the youth's index finger had gone white as it tightened on the trigger. For an eerie split second I was looking at myself from the outside. A kaleidoscope of memory snatches whirled in my mind. The muzzle flash was blinding, and where I was floating, about two feet above the body I no longer owned, a searing hot pain ripped me in two. I died instantly as the aftermath of the shot echoed in the confined space.

The illusion was over. Soaked in cold sweat I looked across the hall to where the Sailor was crouched, screaming incoherently, nursing his shattered right hand.

A few thou of metal had saved my life. The crudely bored out pistol must have exploded when he pulled the trigger. Red and the Kid burst down the stairs and stood staring at the pusher who was spilling blood over the rubble.

I fought back the waves of nausea which turned my legs to jelly.

'Tried to jump me,' I mumbled to the other two. 'You better get out of here. I'll call an ambulance.'

The young pusher was semi-conscious, whimpering in pain. I ran all the way to the telephone. The call was anonymous and it was all I could do to stop my voice shaking. I walked blindly down a couple of streets and was sick over a hedge. Then I went home.

I crept into the house by the back way because I didn't want the neighbours talking. Strange things happened at some of the flats in the district where I lived but my appearance was just too bizarre even for the local non-conformists. I went straight to the bathroom where the wall mirror displayed a glacial hostility. I could see why. The stranger in the glass had unkempt and dirty hair, his forehead was lined with grime and dust-encrusted sweat, and his eyes dulled from lack of sleep had bags like coal sacks underneath. It took half an hour and two razor blades to make my face presentable. Then I soaked in a hot bath.

Afterwards the clean white shirt felt good and I knotted my tie perfectly in the mirror which was speaking to me again.

My stomach was hurting deep down and I dulled the pain with a tot of Dimple Haig from the bottle in the sideboard. Then I walked to a little restaurant around the corner and treated myself to the biggest three-course lunch on the menu.

It was nearly two o'clock when I got to police headquarters. The detective in the CID office told me Cyril was at lunch. I walked to the local boozer. He was sitting in a corner of the smoke room nibbling a cheese sandwich. He looked at me without expression as I sat down opposite him.

'Fancy another one?' I indicated his half-full pint glass.

'No thanks Max. I'm finished. Got to get back in a minute. We're up to our eyes in it across the road.'

I bought myself a half of bitter just to be sociable. Cyril blinked slowly. 'How's the divorce business? Still making a fortune? I reckon I should have put in my ticket long ago and moved to a job with some money in it too,' he said.

'Don't give me that chat, Cyril. You're a dedicated copper. You live and breathe the job. Me, I couldn't stand the routine.'

He looked unamused. I raised my glass and downed the beer.

'There's a little something I want you to do for me, Cyril. It could be to our mutual benefit, but I can't talk here. Can I come with you to the office. It won't take a minute.'

He groaned. 'More screwy ideas I suppose. And I thought you just liked my company.'

I told him he should be on the television making people laugh, and we walked back to the CID in silence. Cyril was obviously nervous as he ushered me into his office and closed the door quickly. We sat on hard-backed chairs facing each other across the table with its miniature PBX, out-of-date calendar, and wire basket bulging with crime reports.

'The gaffer's still a bit prickly over that Leverton business. The fewer people see you, the better. I've still got to work here.' There was apologetic note in Cyril's voice. I sympathized and got down to facts.

'I came across something the other day which I think you ought to know about. I was doing some checking for a client which led me to contact beatniks.'

Cyril cradled his head in his hands and rested his elbows on the table. I ignored his slight groan and continued, 'I treated one of them to a meal because I thought I could get something from him, and he started telling me about a friend of his who was in hospital after taking some new drug which was circulating in the hippy set. He said his friend was very ill and he thought something should be done about it but he was too scared to go to the coppers.'

Cyril cut in, 'What the hell has all this got to do with me. Don't tell me you talked this kid into coming in and you're going to produce him from your back pocket any second.'

'Better than that, he gave me a couple of things, and here's where the favour comes in.'

I delved into my pocket and placed a screw of tissue paper and a plain pill bottle with some liquid in it on the table.

'Can you have the lab run these over for me. I think the result will surprise even you.'

'I'm too old for playing games Max. The boys at the lab are busy, and we don't have time to chase wild theories here, and besides. . . .'

I cut him off. 'Do it as discreetly as possible, and whatever comes of it is yours. If my guess is right, you will be able to nip a full-scale drugs racket in the bud. With a clearance like that, the Home Office will strike a special police medal just for you.'

Cyril thought for a minute. 'Who's this beatnik?' he asked.

'I don't know his name, and anyway you would never trace him now. He's just a drifter.'

'So I do this on the strength of your say so, eh?'

'If you want more, check the hospital. This kid who's sick—I was told his name is Terence St George. Maybe phoney, but it's worth a check. Ask the doctors what he's suffering from and then you'll see I'm levelling with you.'

Cyril looked steadily into my face. 'OK Max, you're a friend of mine, so I'll do it this once. But if it's just a hare-brained stunt, you'll have worn your welcome out here, understand?'

'Fair enough,' I said and stood up. He sat staring at the two objects on the table.

'I don't suppose you want to tell me who your client is Max?' he asked softly.

'You know better than that Cyril.' I closed the door quietly and went out into the sunshine.

9

When the telephone rang next morning, I was still in bed. It was Cyril to say that the lab had analysed the powder without wasting any time. They had a result and he wanted to see me straight away. He said it in an official tone of voice, so I was at the Central Police Station within half an hour, giving my name and being ushered into an upstairs office by a police constable. Cyril was there but he wasn't alone. With him was a stocky man of about forty-five who wore steel-rimmed glasses. Sitting in a chair in another corner of the room was another man, dark, tall, perhaps a year or two older than myself.

'Max, this is Mr Claybuck of the Regional Forensic Science Laboratory. That's Inspector Bland of the Narcotics Intelligence Squad.'

I nodded and Cyril pointed to a chair. I sat down and Claybuck sat down too. Cyril was the first to speak.

'Are you sure you've told us all you know about where this powder came from?'

I nodded. 'Yes, off a beat as I said. Don't know his name. He was choked because his friend was in hospital. He talked about it when I stood him a meal. He seemed to think his friend had got ill through taking that powder. That's all I know.'

'I wish I could believe you Max. This is important. I don't see what you've got to gain by being awkward and you know all about the penalties for withholding information.'

'Certainly, that's why I wouldn't do it. Anyway I brought the powder in and I've told you all I know. I'd very much like to know what it is.'

'Why?'

'Curiosity. It's nothing to do with the investigation I was on Cyril. That's over anyway. You never know I might remember more while you're talking.'

Cyril grimaced and then nodded to Claybuck. The scientist leaned forward.

'Yes. This is an organic drug of a peculiarly pernicious type. It has an effect rather akin to amphetamine when taken in small quantities: it is merely a stimulant. It is unusual because it is not easily broken down in the body which can excrete only a limited amount. Once that amount is exceeded, it builds up in the intestines and blood stream, and once a certain concentration is reached—depending on the physical size of the taker—its effect changes not only in degree but in kind. It has a complex effect on the autonic and central nervous systems. Put simply, it becomes an hallucinatory drug of the most potent kind. Its effects then are not unlike those of lysergic acid, except that for some reason as yet unknown, the nature of the experiences the taker goes through are more variable. He can either become insanely happy and think he is more alive than ever before or, and this happens more if the drug is taken unawares, he can suffer great agonies of mind.'

I blinked. 'Oh. Is this a new discovery?'

'No. Scientists have known about the existence of this compound for a long time, but it has no use whatever medically because its effects are at the moment unpredictable and uncontrollable. It is also extremely difficult to isolate in a completely pure state and that brings further complications.'

Cyril cut in. 'So you see it is vitally important that we trace the source of this drug. If it gets into the hands of youngsters it's a killer. That kid in the hospital died early this morning.'

Dragon was dead. I felt the blood drain from my face. Cyril couldn't have missed it either.

'All right. Did you find what was in the bottle I brought in?'

Claybuck looked puzzled. 'Eh, yes. It was merely a soap liquid of some kind. We broke it down completely. These commercial products are never pure, but it didn't seem unusual.'

'Wouldn't it be possible to get the drug from the liquid?'

Claybuck paused and looked at me with slightly narrowed eyes. He pulled a wad of notes from his inside pocket and laid them on the desk. He looked at Cyril and nodded minutely.

'In this liquid apart from all the usual stearates there is an organic hydrocarbon compound. It's there to make the liquid feel more silky to the touch. Good for advertising purposes I suppose. It has no effect on the washing properties but it might help to keep a housewife's hands feeling more soft I suppose—you know the sort of thing,' he said.

'And the drug comes from that?'

'No. Not exactly. In fact theoretically this compound is quite stable and doesn't react with any of the other constituents of the liquid. But the fact is it can have a reaction with one of the stearates. The products are less stable than the reagents and it decomposes back to the original reagents again at normal temperatures.'

'At normal temperatures?'

Claybuck smiled slightly. 'You have an analytical mind. If this liquid is refrigerated to a temperature well below freezing point, when the hydrocarbon and stearate react the resulting organic chemical becomes more stable. Not altogether stable but stable enough for some to be obtained from the solution.'

'Would that be easy?'

'Unfortunately yes. Chemically it would be almost impossible. But as it happens this drug, which is the result, is insoluble. It precipitates and therefore physical isolation is quite simple. Of course it's far from pure.'

My eyebrows went up. 'OK, Cyril, the fact is that liquid is Sluico. You can buy it in any supermarket.'

Bland was out of his chair and through the door before I could say another word.

Cyril took out a large handkerchief and mopped his brow.

'That'll cut down our problem to some extent. We've got the lab going through every commercial soap liquid on the market checking for this thing. How did you know?'

'A lucky guess. I hate to reopen old wounds, mate. Battersby worked for the Sluico manufacturers. His briefcase was missing remember? I told you I'd keep working on that. I reckon this is why he was killed.'

Cyril glanced hurriedly at Claybuck and back to me.

'What else do you know?'

'Nothing. A colleague of Battersby's told me about this. I did some snooping around the city's junkies. You know the rest. I found this drug and played a hunch as to the Sluico.'

'Right, well stay here. I'm going to see Ralph Grey. We've got to put a stop to this stuff coming on the market in its present state.'

Cyril and Claybuck left the room. I thought. That tank in the cellar had been a refrigerator of some kind. I sat there for about twenty minutes before Cyril came back. He had Ralph Grey with him.

Grey sat down opposite me. He didn't introduce himself, just fixed his eyes on me and opened up.

'Mr Daly, we are now arranging for the manufacturers to halt all supplies of Sluico to retailers. We are arranging the recall of all existing stocks as far as possible and we are going to make sure none of this is sold until the offending compound is eliminated from the formula.'

I broke in. 'Will this become public?'

'We'll take damn good care to see that it does not. Sluico obviously won't be too keen to publicize it. It would do their position a great deal of harm. We are keeping it from the public to prevent the possibility of more people extracting their own drug from existing Sluico bottles in circulation.'

I was going to say something, but he cut me off.

'Now Mr Daly, I needn't tell you that in spite of all this, there is quite enough of this liquid about to enable a lot of this drug to be made. You can see, I am sure, that it is extremely marketable to drug takers and addicts because it can be sold to all sorts. To some it can be sold merely as a pep drug and it can also be sold to others as a hard drug. If taken to excess by people unprepared it can cause violent hallucinations and result in death.'

I had nothing to say.

'Now Mr Daly, Chief Inspector McClellan tells me he's not entirely satisfied with your co-operation in this matter.'

This time I wasn't impressed and I didn't mind if he found out:

'Look Mr Grey, let's not forget who found this drug. I don't want any medals or anything but I do rather object to being interrogated. There's no question of my trying to conceal anything from the police. I've told you what I know.'

He gave me the sort of look usually reserved for things you find under cabbage leaves in wet weather, but he said nothing.

'But there is something I should like to know.' A pause. 'You know why I was fooling around with drugs anyway. Because Battersby worked for Sluico and his briefcase was missing. Would you mind telling me what the CID view is now about that?'

Grey's last look was one of mute adoration compared to the one he'd switched on now.

'It's a series of interesting coincidences. We'll probably look into it, but there's no question of there being enough evidence to warrant a re-opening of the inquest.'

I raised an eyebrow.

'There is still a lot of evidence to say Leverton killed Battersby. Now you'd better understand that my previous advice still holds good. This is police business and it doesn't improve through being complicated by amateurs—even lucky amateurs,' he added.

I nodded.

'Was it Thorpe-Winman who told you about Battersby's drug work?'

'That's right. But I don't think he was trying to conceal it before. I got him drunk. He'd forgotten all about it. Didn't think it was significant. In fact he didn't even realize it mattered when he told me. He just let it slip in a happy mood.'

Grey looked unimpressed. My patter left Thorpe-Winman a slight chance. It was up to him to lie his way out of the rest of it.

'Well, next time you find such a thing out, it's always best to tell us before doing anything flashy.'

Again I nodded. Then I stood up and took my leave. Cyril shook his head ever so slightly as I reached the door. Grey just looked at me woodenly.

10

At dusk I went to the Club Cabana. It was early and the bar was almost empty. A couple of paunchy businessmen were propping up the far corner of the copper-topped semi-circle probably waiting for the gambling to hot up. A muscular young man was taking a rest from 'bouncer duty' lounging with his elbows on the bar. The barman sidled across to me and said good evening in a broad Birmingham accent. I asked for a large whisky with ice, and he was soon back with the drink which he set in front of me. I was about to speak to him again when I realized someone was standing by my right shoulder; someone a little taller and a little broader than myself, someone with warm breath that suggested spicy eating. The incredible Mr Smith.

'How are you Mr Daly? Haven't seen you or our mutual friend Mr Thorpe-Winman around lately. I was beginning to think our little club was becoming unpopular.'

Smith looked down at his fingernails. I put my hands in my pockets and turned to face him. 'Hello Mr Smith,' I said.

He spread his legs slightly and smiled slowly, his tombstone teeth glinting in the subdued light.

'I don't suppose you've seen Roy lately, either?'

'Not since I saw you before.'

Smith sneered. 'No, he didn't seem to be a promising friend. Have a pleasant evening.'

He turned abruptly, nodded to the barman who had been waiting at a respectful distance, and strode across the room past the ankle-high tables and black leather chairs, and through the alcove into the Chemin de fer room where play was starting to hum. I ordered another drink and spoke to the barman, 'Quiet tonight. Has everyone in town run out of money?'

He was polishing a glass which didn't need polishing.

'This time of the week, it's always a quiet night. Makes a change from the week-end. Gives us a chance to take a breather.'

The young bouncer had gone about his duties, and the two men from the city were enjoying the conversation of a curvacious hostess in a low-cut dress who was, after all, being paid to be nice.

The barman had quite an amusing line in idle chatter, and I didn't notice the woman come into the bar. She was talking to a distinguished-looking, grey-haired man and I recognized her immediately as the woman I had seen on my first visit to the Cabana.

I leaned towards the barman and spoke quietly:
'Who's that?'
'Friend of the gaffer.'
'Mr Tait?'
'Ar. That's right.'
'What's her name?'

The barman grinned. 'Fancy her do you? Her name's Mrs Ragas. You'll be all right if you've got a couple of yachts floating in your private lake, sort of thing.'

I grimaced. 'A skiff at the park is more my style.'

As we talked the grey-haired man left. Here was a chance to meet someone named Ragas, a name in which I had a professional interest. I walked across to where she sat and put my my drink down on the table.

'May I join you? I know we haven't been introduced. I was just wondering who could do it for us.'

She smiled patiently as if she had been in that situation before.

I grinned. 'I hope you're not offended.'

She laughed shortly. 'Not quite. Are you often so adventurous with women in bars?'

I shrugged and sat sown. 'Only when they're beautiful, and then I usually fail.'

'Good gracious—an honest man. But thank you for the compliment.' She smiled over her empty glass.

'Would you like another drink?' I asked.

'Well thank you.' She paused and added ironically, 'I feel I should be wearing a bunny costume.'

I laughed. 'Then I would have to go on to iced water.'

'Well, I'd prefer an Italian white vermouth.'

The barman set the drinks in front of us, gave me no change from half a sheet, and retired to the bar with a knowing look.

Mrs Ragas was beautiful. She wore a black evening dress that showed off her full upper arms and smooth shoulders.

'My name's Daly. Maxwell Daly. Friends call me Max.'

'I won't ask whose friends. How do you do Max. I'm Myfanwy Ragas.'

'You're Welsh?'

'No, my mother was. I was born in Peterborough but she got her way in our family, at least as far as names were concerned.'

I wondered how a woman-dominated family could produce anything so superbly feminine, but I didn't say so. I was so busy looking at the translucent eyes with their great suggestion of depth, and the way her dark hair framed her face that I entirely missed her next remark.

'Sorry?'

'I was asking what you did, and I do wish you wouldn't stare like that.'

'Oh. I'm sorry I stare.'

I stared.

'You don't look very sorry and it doesn't matter if you don't want to tell me how you spend your time.'

'Well I'm not sorry from my point of view, of course. As a matter of fact, I'm a private detective.'

She looked inquiring and half-incredulous. Then when I nodded she gave a quick little smile.

'Are you off duty or on now?'

'Oh, completely off duty.'

She looked a little coldly and remarked that it must be awfully exciting. You could see she didn't really think so.

'Not in the least. It's rather depressing. It's been a nice day hasn't it?'

At that she laughed.

She didn't want to talk about herself although she talked freely enough about her interests and things in general. After a few more drinks I began to feel reckless.

'You know I could tell you weren't thoroughly Anglo-Saxon.'

'Oh?'

'Mm. You have too much appreciation of your own attraction. You accept it matter of factly without unnecessary embarrassment or reserve.'

She smiled slowly. 'I think you are a dangerous man.'

I felt a little pleased in spite of myself but I didn't show it. 'Nonsense. I'm completely disarmed already.'

The evening flew and at two she had to go. I offered her a lift but she had a car of her own. I fetched her coat and helped her on with it, and then offered to walk her to her car, but she said she'd come with an old friend who by now would have lost his shirt in one of the gaming rooms. As she turned to go, I spoke, 'I've enjoyed this evening.'

'Yes, it's been nice.'

'I'd like to see you again.'

She looked at me. Her expression was slightly sad. 'You know I'm married,' she said, dropping her eyes towards her left hand.

'What about tomorrow evening? We could take a drive into the country unless you would prefer dinner and the theatre.'

She nodded. 'The country will be fine.'

Her stately posture disappeared. She looked at me with a sultry expression from behind a frond of hair that had tipped across her face. 'I'll meet you at seven at the "Cosmopolitan". Don't be late. I hate to be kept waiting by a man.'

Her lips parted in a quick smile, then she was gone.

*

The 'Cosmopolitan' was a coffee-house full of maiden ladies until five o'clock, empty until eight o'clock, and then full of teenagers.

Mrs Ragas swung into the place when I had been there some time. She threaded her way through the tables to join me and I had plenty of time to notice the orange lipstick which matched the orange silk scarf she was shaking from her hair. The suede jacket she was wearing could not have cost less than a hundred and fifty guineas and looked straight out of the Tyrol. We said hello and went out to my car.

There was a slight constraint between us as I moved out into the traffic and headed out of town, as if having embarked on an escapade in the bright lights of the Cabana last night, she was now wondering why. And as for me, I wasn't sure how to begin finding out what she knew about her husband's affairs.

The evening rush period had died and soon we were racing out along an arterial road to the south. It had been a fine day. The sun was sinking to our right in a congealed explosion of red. Above its flare, the sky clung greenish yellow and elsewhere opened in a limitless expanse of deepening blue. In the livid evening light buildings and trees were sharply delineated. The tyres hummed on the road. I grinned.

'What's the matter?'

'Don't know, just feel good. I must be a poetic soul at heart.'

She smiled. 'A likely story.'

The country inn was as quiet as I hoped it would be. A few locals sat around the bar, but in the lounge with its wooden beams and little unexpected alcoves, there wasn't a soul. When we had got out of the car on the desert of shale that was the car park and listened to the crickets, there had been a slight nip in the evening air. But inside there was a low log fire. In the country, Mrs Ragas drank beer.

The thaw came as we sat in the old room and listened to a distant radio play quietly to itself. The burr of the country voices, the distant music, the crackling of the fire, the good beer which slipped down, all went to create an intimate atmosphere.

She asked for my life story. I told her I had knocked around a bit in my youth, drifted into private investigation when hired by an old-timer with an aversion to ex-policemen, and I was now rather a lonely and misunderstood soul. It wasn't a bad spiel. Mrs Ragas listened sympathetically but changed the subject when I asked her about herself. Eventually we got back to me.

'I've been seriously thinking about giving up my present line. Your time's not your own and it hardly leaves you with a sense of satisfaction at the end of the day.'

'What would you do?'

'That's the whole point. What indeed? I'm not really qualified for anything else where I could support myself in the style to which I am unaccustomed.'

'That's always the trouble.'

She sounded almost bitter, so I probed a little further. 'Don't try and tell me you have any troubles,' I laughed.

She just smiled again and said nothing. It was a thing she did a lot.

The evening ebbed to its end, and at closing time we went back to the car. I got in first and opened her door. She leaned out of the darkness into the illuminated little world of the car's saloon. She sat down and swung her beautiful strong woman's legs in after her. My right arm lay on the steering wheel. I was half-turned towards her.

'How do you close this door?'

I leaned across her, grabbed the armrest and slammed the door shut. As I did so her lips ran gently over my left ear, sending a dwarf with cold feet running around my neck and marching down my spine. One of her hands moved to my back and squashed the dwarf as he went. I straightened, slipping my arm around her. My other hand caressed the back of her neck and I kissed her gently. Then the hand spread over her hair and pulled her head hard into mine. She liked it. She made me like it and I lost track of the time.

When my hand strayed towards her breast she spoke softly. 'Where can we go Max?'

'My place?'

'Please.'

She didn't take her eyes off me as we drove back quickly. The speed of this development surprised me a little, but I wasn't exactly breaking my heart about it. I ran the car into the drive silently and we got out. I was fumbling with my key when she stood in front of me. Her legs were braced, there was a slight curl to her lip, her perfect teeth flashed. She snapped a finger into my chest. 'Listen Max Daly. Don't try and tell me you're a little ship lost in the storm. I don't believe it.'

Her hand ran up to my neck. I pressed her into the angle of the door and we kissed savagely. When we broke off she froze with her head back. A funny smile combining sensuality and self-satisfaction was on her face. I turned the key, pushed open the door and hustled her in front of me. She had me thinking now and I knew it wouldn't do to underestimate her. I switched on the lamp and the room looked yellow and dingy in its sixty-watt light. I made a mental note to get a more powerful bulb. She didn't seem to notice the drabness. She stood in the middle of my carpet with her head on one side. 'So this is Joyous Gard?'

I laughed. 'The name was Daly not Launcelot—'

'Let me guess—your armour is all rusty from rescuing damsels in the rain.'

We both laughed. I took two steps towards her and slipped my arms loosely round her waist.

She put her forefinger on my lips.

'How about some coffee . . . ?' she asked.
'Sure you wouldn't prefer a drink?'
'Coffee will be fine.'

I sighed, and left her. In the kitchen I plugged in the electric kettle and thumbed the switch.

Through the open door I saw her pick up a book from my untidy shelf. Leaning against the door frame she leafed it idly. She didn't really look too interested in *Moriarty's Police Law*. I poured the coffee and took two cups back into the room. She sauntered ahead of me and pushed a door opposite. It opened to reveal my bedroom.

'Here's the coffee,' I said.

'Coffee—at a time like this?' Her voice had a mocking quality.

Her eloquent hips swayed as she moved towards me. A glacier slipped icily into the pit of my stomach.

I swept her up and into the bedroom. She was laughing and calling me a beast.

I dropped her lightly on to her feet; our lips coalesced as I unzipped her dress. The smooth cream of her shoulders would have taken my breath away if I'd had any to spare. She shimmered from her slip. Its silk was no smoother than her skin gleaming in the half-dark. On the floor *Moriarty's* pages fluttered.

My palms smoothed, caressed, played with, then gripped her breasts through the blackness of her brassiere. 'Take it off,' she breathed.

I remember her body tightening against mine. I remember we fell on to the bed. I remember. . . .

It was not very sweet. It wasn't very tender. It was plain animal. I lay on the bed gingerly fingering the bites on my shoulder, enjoying the pounding in my chest and the ache in my loins. She was lying beside me, a damp wisp of hair sticking to her forehead.

She looked sad and turned over on to her stomach. My eyes languished on the cute roundness above her thighs.

She didn't speak straight away, but looked earnestly

across the curve of her right shoulder. 'I had to Max. It's been so long. . . .'

My eyebrows lifted in surprise. 'Hubby?'

'God him! He's impotent,' she said flatly.

I looked at my watch. It was well past one. Her eyes followed my arm. 'I'll have to go Max. I'm sorry.' And a few minutes later she slipped from the bed and stood running her hands through her hair.

In the oblique light slanting from the doorway she reached for her clothes. Her breasts were firm and neat. Her thighs were long with the slight swelling of muscle. She saw I was looking at her.

'Do you like my body?'

'It's all right. A bit low-slung in the undercarriage, but built for bed-work I'd say.'

She scooped up *Moriarty* and hurled it at my head.

'Men are so crude sometimes,' she said, strolling out of the room.

The Ragas household where I dropped her was a rambling, white-fronted mansion on the reverse slope of the Lickey Hills near Barnt Green. The long drive wound through beechwoods to the house.

I left her at the porch. There was no traffic, but it still took half an hour to drive home.

11

The heavy morning traffic slowed down my trip to Nechells. Sam Snape was alone in the tiny barber's shop marked by the peeling striped pole. He was a little man, with sharp, rodent-like features and patent leather hair, wearing an immaculate white coat with a couple of vicious cut-throats in the breast pocket.

'Wotcher Max. Long time, no see.'

'Just a trim Sam, and a little chat. What's moving on the patch?'

'There ain't much and that's a fact. All the best villains are in the nick. It's this new bleedin' crime squad. Hot as mustard they are. I tell you straight, an honest villain can't make a decent living no more.'

I steered the conversation around to the hi-jacking of the Sluico lorry.

'Now that one has really got me beat. The busies haven't got a smell of that job. Meself, I don't think it was professionals. No self-respecting heister is going to snatch a lot of bloody washing-up stuff, now is he? Fags is different. We ain't had a good fags haul in a long time. Just petty stuff.'

Sam sounded rather wistful about the lack of enterprise and I asked him if there was any indication of London gangs moving in or any new rackets developing.

'No mate. The lads from the Smoke 'ave a bash now and then. The jelly boys and the payroll merchants used to come up the motorway but the coppers scared 'em off. Too clever by half some of these youngsters, yer know—they'd nick their own grannies, straight up.'

Sam assured me he would have heard if there was something in the wind, but he didn't know about drugs. 'Ain't my kind of caper, see. Leave that to the spades. A nice, clean bank job or a wagon full of fags, then you're talking.'

He promised to call me if he heard anything and said

he would put out a few feelers to see if a new drugs ring was operating, but he made it clear that he didn't relish the idea although I was a friend of long standing. Sam was my best informer and he kept me in close touch with the city's underworld. I slipped him a quid and left the shop. Little bits of hair were prickling under my collar.

About mid-morning I went to the nearest library and looked up Kelly's street directory of Birmingham. From it I learned that Tarrasch was tenanted by a Mr N. N. Edwards. I went back to the car and went out to Edgbaston. I was just hoping that the boys organizing the basement druggery had not taken fright and cleared out. I drove slowly down the street and in daylight it looked more dilapidated and faded than before. Tarrasch wore the same air of rambling gloom. It looked about as lived-in as it had before and there were no 'to let' signs in the front garden.

As for N. N. Edwards, that could have been an alias, or else the man could have been clean. At any rate I had no access to MID-CRO where the answer was sure to be, and the name meant nothing to policemen I spoke to in the boozer at lunch time.

12

I lay in bed and watched the ceiling. The alarm had just gone and I supposed I would have to get up, but the soft warmth of the sheets had a charm I reckoned it would take me a quarter of an hour to overcome. Recollections of the previous evening floated through my head taking the attention I should have directed to keeping my eyelids apart. It had been quite a pleasant evening. The drive to the big house, and the arrival, the attractive Mrs Ragas appearing at the door, the play which had been quite amusing. Dinner, too, had been a definite success. Myfanwy wore a low, sleeveless dress and black jet ear-rings that contrasted with the creamy skin of her neck.

Conversation had been unforced but I discovered no more about Ragas. After I drove her home, I kissed her and watched her slip through the large front door with a little wave of her hand. There was no sex that night. She was showing me that she wasn't that easy.

My daydreams became real dreams as I dozed again, until I woke with a start and shook the fuzziness from my head. Then I tumbled out of bed before I went to sleep again, and languidly dressed for the office.

The pigeons were numerous that day. They perched fussily on the ledges and cornices of the buildings I could see from the window of my office on the fourth floor. I tilted back in my old leather swivel chair and rested my heels on the blotter on my desk.

Dust particles danced in a shaft of sunlight from outside. I threw the morning paper on to the top of my solitary filing cabinet to join a pile of yellowing papers. As it landed in a puff of dust the telephone rang. The cool voice of Mrs Leverton spoke from the other end of the line.

'This affair has been on my mind much more than I had expected, Mr Daly. When you called, and after the divorce I just wanted to forget it all but time has gone on and I find I'm curious to know if you've discovered anything.'

So I told her about the drugs being manufactured in the house in Edgbaston and the connexion with Battersby. That could provide a motive for the killing on the train, but I didn't know any more.

'Have you told the police?'

'I've told them some of it.'

'Is it wise not to tell them everything?'

'It's probably downright foolish as a matter of fact but if they step in before I can link Mr Leverton with the affair, the only lead will have gone.'

'So you're going to persist with the inquiry?'

'It would seem rather pointless to stop now.'

For a moment there was no answer. Then she said hesistatingly, 'Yes, well you know I'd like to know. And our arrangement stands.'

'Yeah sure. Thanks for ringing.'

There was a click as she hung up. Holding the speechless receiver for a moment I reflected that women are peculiar creatures.

*

Myfanwy and I had afternoon tea in the 'Cosmopolitan', then we went to a film and afterwards back to my place where she cooked me a meal. We looked at each other over the coffee and talked for some time. During lulls in the conversation, she percolated more coffee and poured it into my cup. She began to tell me about herself for the first time. She was wearing a plain, turquoise dress with a high neck and no sleeves. Her hair was loose and she wore no make-up. Her only jewellery was a thick bronze bracelet.

She spoke softly. 'I was just a kid in Peterborough Max. God if only you knew how dull that town was.'

We both laughed. I reached out and held her hand, running my thumb gently over her palm.

'Paul Ragas?'

'My, I thought he was God at that time I can tell you.

My mother was a strict nonconformist you know and I never did find out what my father was. It didn't make much difference anyway. I went to a local girl's school for the lower middle-class with aspirations.

'You know it was a girls' only school and of course the atmosphere at home wasn't conducive to boy friends. I never went out with a boy until I was twenty. By then I suppose my romantic illusions had grown to such an extent that I was dissatisfied with any boy I got. They all fell short of some other girl's fellow or the Galahads of my imagination. One year there was a month's school trip to America and I went. I absolutely fell in love with the place. It seemed to be the hub of the universe somehow . . . all that enormous vitality.'

'Never been. It hasn't ever appealed to me much. I have this exaggerated impression of a barely-civilized, mechanized jungle peopled by uncultured bigots.'

She laughed, 'Sounds like Birmingham.'

'Touché.'

'No, Max, I think any place is lovely if you're happy—even Peterborough. We just project our mood on to the poor town. I've never been to Stockton. I imagine it's beautiful if you have a pleasant circle of friends and a good lover there.'

'What did you do in America?'

'Oh, well while we were there I went with one of the girls who was a friend of mine to visit an uncle and aunt of her's in New York. Well I think they saw how hopelessly starry-eyed about the place I was and they were flattered. Between ourselves I think uncle had also taken a sort of fancy to me as well.

'Anyway on our return to England my friend arranged to spend six months with them and I was invited too. Mother didn't like the idea of course but she was flattered by the social status of Julie's—that's my friend's—people and after they cajoled her, she agreed. Father who was ill then anyway rubber stamped the decision and there it was.

'I was almost twenty then and I began to meet lots of

men. I was out every night. At the end of the six months I took a job in a travel bureau office. That's where I met Paul Ragas. I suppose he picked me up.

'God, to me he was the ultimate, greying slightly even then. He's bald now of course. He was stocky but not fat like now. I suppose I was a bit wild. I put superficial sophistication above most things. The very word morality was anathema to me after what I'd been through at home. People told me Paul was not altogether the most socially acceptable of men but that just made him more desirable in my eyes. That's how it happened.'

'And now you're back here?'

'Huh. Yes. I prefer England now. It's just as well I do. Paul was getting edged out of Detroit, sandwiched between some big mobsters and the law. He thought British gambling was just right for a smooth entrepreneur as he calls it, and the nomadic Ragases were on the move again.'

She jumped up and went to the sink.

'Never mind the dishes, they'll keep.'

'Now come on Max, then we'll have the whole evening to ourselves.'

'Quite the little suburban housewife at heart aren't you?'

I put my head through the kitchen door and withdrew it hurriedly as a tea towel sang across the kitchen and slapped into the wall.

'Truce?'

'All right you big booby you can come in. But you can wash and I'll dry for that.'

We flopped on the couch afterwards. And we made love. Afterwards I said I wished it had been me in the travel bureau. She looked pained.

'I didn't think you'd get corny.'

'I feel corny. It was best that time.'

She grinned, rolled towards me and slipped her hand down my stomach.

'Mmmmmm. Potential fulfilled. It was like a flame that swelled through my whole body until I wasn't really conscious.'

'Aren't I entitled to a little corn then?'

'I suppose so. Just didn't think it was you in a way.'

'Look, Myfanwy, we're not adolescents who overcompliment so they can have their egos boosted by the nice things said back to them. The trouble with me is that I've got a big streak of conformity which I can't entirely stifle. And I hate to think of you going back in the morning to him.'

She slipped both hands up suddenly and cupped them around my chin.

'Oh darling, don't even think about that.'

Suddenly she shuddered and her eyes became luminous.

'I hate that bastard. If you really want to know, I hate him.'

'But. . . .'

'There are no buts Max. I loathe and detest him more than I can ever say. We don't sleep together now . . . not even the same room. And I'm glad . . . I'm bloody glad.'

I grabbed her clumsily and cradled her head on my chest. There was a moment's silence before she looked up with a wry grin. Her eyes were still bright. There was no sign of tears.

'Now I've let myself down.'

'Don't be stupid. I understand.'

'No you don't, darling. How can you? He's more than a bit shady. He's a sadist. Nothing he did would surprise me. I don't know what I feel about you really, but God do I regret the day I ever laid eyes on Paul Ragas or any of that bunch.'

Nothing more was said. We lay down in each other's arms and soon she was asleep. I lay awake thinking. Then I too dozed off only to be awakened by her insistence. I slept afterwards and when I awoke I felt cold. A grey early morning light paled the window behind the drawn curtains. We had parted in sleep and her smooth back was towards me. One arm above the bedclothes. She stirred and looked at me sleepily. There was mischief in her face. I didn't know how she felt about me. I knew she hated Ragas. That was no act. And time was running out for me.

13

She gurgled in sleepy amusement. My grin lacked conviction.

'Mmmmmm. Why so serious?'

'I was thinking about what you said.'

Her face became interrogative, then darkened.

'Last night?'

'Yes.'

'Oh do we have to talk about it, darling?'

Again I grinned and let myself slide down until my face was about two inches from hers.

'Sorry.'

Her hands slipped around me again. This was a woman who just didn't stop. She was playing about now, running her wet lips over my face and rubbing my nose with her own.

'Naughty,' she said, 'you're not trying.'

'I'm never at my best when my mind is working.'

'Turn it off then.'

'Wish I could.'

She frowned and pushed my face back with her index finger.

'It's come to me, sweetie, that you can help me, but I don't like to ask. It might make you think something that isn't true.'

She frowned again. The frown not of a cultivated woman, but a petulant girl disturbed while playing with a favourite toy.

'Promise you'll be nice to me and I don't expect I'll get very upset. You don't look very down and out.'

Now there was a slight but perceptible caution in her manner.

'Nothing like that. Sometime ago I fell down on a job that might have concerned your husband.' She froze suddenly.

'You want information don't you?'
'Not if it means interfering with us.'
'Well?' She didn't say it with any enthusiasm. I feared that I had seriously overplayed my hand but I had given her the patter and couldn't turn back now. 'It's about murder,' I said.

Her brow knitted.

'It was a murder over a drug racket I think. I believe your husband was involved.'

Her manner was severe. She was sitting up looking at me with a mixture of disbelief and distaste. 'How do you imagine he was involved?'

So I told her about the two deaths, and Battersby's discovery of the drug, and about its circulation in the city. I didn't tell her why I thought Ragas was involved; it wasn't necessary. She sat up in bed but didn't look shocked, but then I hadn't expected her to be entirely ignorant of her husband's business activities.

'Well?' she said.

'Leverton ought not to be held responsible for those deaths.'

'So much ought not to happen. It does. So what?'

'I think your husband was responsible. I'm sorry, but I do.'

'You've been using me haven't you?'

'No, God no, sweetie. You should know better than that. That's why I was at the Cabana I admit, but I made a pass at you before I knew who you were. Look I loathe this crummy job. I wouldn't pass up anything like you . . . or this . . . for it. If you're disgusted or don't want to know, forget it.'

There was a moment's silence. Then I spoke again.

'But you can't forget it can you? Neither can I. This is why I hate your going back to him, not for any sentimental bourgeois moral reasons. Because he's a killer, by proxy if not in fact, because you must know that he is, because it would always be a constraint between us if I didn't speak out.'

She looked at me soberly out of those big, brown, liquid eyes. Her face was as wooden as a ceremonial mask. But much more beautiful.

'And what? I don't ask questions about what he's doing. That's elementary self-defence I suppose. It's nothing to do with me anyway. I just thought he was here for the gambling. That's what I want to think. . . . I'd better go.'

I grabbed her and kissed her hard. It would have been quite a good kiss. I did my best but you can't cause much of a flutter when her mouth is tightly closed and she's rigid with passive resistance. I released her and looked at her sadly. Then she gave an odd little shrug and looked down at where my hand lay on the sheet two inches from her own.

'What is there to be done, Max? It's hopeless isn't it?'

I grabbed her again and held her away from me, staring at her flushed face.

'It doesn't have to be. I don't care how we go on as long as we do somehow. I don't care what he does, but this . . . I can't take the murder of people I know. I can be as conveniently blind as anyone else. He can do what he likes but I can't stomach this. Help me to put this one right and we can forget the rest.'

Silence.

'I couldn't ask if it weren't you, Myfanwy.'

She tore herself from me and looked away. She stared at the curtains, but she didn't attempt to go.

'What the hell do you want me to do?' she said suddenly. 'Turn him in for murder? For God's sake I don't love the bastard but he is my husband. Anyway I couldn't open my mouth without getting us both . . . killed or something.'

'No. You know better than that, sweetie. There'll be no question of his being charged. He won't be connected anyway. But if we can just fix it so his minions who did it get the blame. That'll be all right won't it? Then we'll go on in any way you want.'

'Why does it matter to you?'

'Because I want to go on . . . . any way you want. And I can't while we know this.'

'Oh hell, Max, you're mad. What can we possibly do to make it like that?'

She turned to me, still frowning, but no longer a frown of perplexity, now of worry, sorrow, almost of appeal, or so I thought.

'I don't know. I'm no genius. The only thing I can think of . . . is that briefcase, the one I told you about. The one that's missing. If you could find out where that is and get it . . .'

Her eyes closed and opened slowly. She shook her head.

'Oh, Max. You don't know what you're asking.'

'Perhaps not. But if I knew where it was, if I could get it. It might at least clear Leverton. Ragas can look after himself. He'd just have to cut a couple of his boys adrift.'

'Do you think he could get away with that?'

'Why not? There's no death penalty here. They'd get a long sentence in jail. They'd keep quiet. Better jail than a broken skull after all.'

'What is it you want?'

'See if you can find out about that briefcase. If you can't do it without endangering yourself, don't do it. If you find out, don't try and get it, just tell me.'

She looked at me for a minute or so. She looked rather strained and she didn't say anything. Then she blinked and nodded dumbly. I kissed her, held her close and comforted her. But there was no love-making after that. How could there be?

14

When she left I felt rather flat, as any good professional does when he has just given of his best. She refused to let me drive her but said she was going into town and would catch a bus. The walking would help to clear her mind.

Yet later when I drove into town and went to the office I felt better. At least it felt as if I was trying to make things happen again. The sense of drift was eased and this improved my mood. When the day came to an end I had heard nothing, but that didn't really worry me because I knew these things would take time.

Next morning, however, the feeling of drift was back. I couldn't hang about doing nothing even if I did have an iron in the fire. Sitting by my breakfast table, I wondered if Grey's drug probe was getting anywhere. If, perhaps, it might lead to the police doing my work for me. I considered paying a visit to Thorpe-Winman at the Sluico Chemical place to see if he had been bothered again and to see if he could tell me anything more.

The telephone call changed all that. It was Myfanwy. The STD pips said she was calling from a public telephone box. I never did find out which one.

Her voice was polite and passionless.

'This is about what you wanted to know.'

'Eh! That was quick. I didn't expect to hear so soon about it.'

'The briefcase you want is at the house in Barnt Green.'

'My God that's lucky! How did you find out so quickly? Is it safe to talk?'

'Do you really care?'

'Oh hell, sweetie, we can't talk about that over a telephone. You must know I do. Don't you trust me at all?'

She said it was safe for her to talk. She didn't know what was in the briefcase, she only knew where it was and that it was the one I wanted. She wasn't going to tell me how she had found out. Not then anyway.

The briefcase, Battersby's briefcase, was in a wall safe in the library at Barnt Green. The room was oak panelled with shelves and busts and a desk, and she told me how to get to it. She also told me the combination of the safe.

'What about people in the house?'

'My husband is still at the town flat. I shall be out for the evening . . . with a friend. I'll give all the staff the night off. There will be a french window open at the side of the house. It opens into the hall. I've told you the way from there.'

'Myfanwy. I do see you after that don't I?'

'Oh,' she said almost impatiently, 'I don't know Max. That is . . . it's up to you I suppose.'

'I'll let you know how I get on. Where can I contact you?'

'Never mind. I'll ring you when it's all right for me to do it.'

'All right, sweetie. And thanks. I can't tell you. . . .'

'No,' she said, more resigned than bitter. ''Bye.'

The phone clicked. My heart was pounding with anticipation. It could be the beginning of the end of the whole affair. How had that amazing woman found out?—it was unbelievable luck. In fact it was too lucky in a way, but I didn't think about that. I was eager for a quick resolution. Perhaps I'm not patient enough to be a private operator.

The excursion to Barnt Green had to be staged at just about midnight, I reasoned, so I began to get things ready—gloves, torch, moccasin shoes and a slip of paper with the safe combination on it. I had a strange lack of appetite so I skipped tea and spent most of the early evening in a pub. It was after eleven o'clock when I went to the car and I could not resist the temptation to drive quickly so I arrived in the area before midnight, earlier than I had planned.

The Lickey Hills are Birmingham's proletarian playground south-west of the city. The road that goes past Rednal winds under the ridge on to Barnt Green in the Bromsgrove Rural

District. To the right is Lickey and the road to Bromsgrove via Blackwell leads past many a shady drive to the houses of the very rich indeed.

Chez Ragas was set in sloping parkland dotted with oak and beech. The road has just left the conurbation when it passes the entrance to their drive and is narrow and rather quiet. At eleven forty-five it is quieter than at most other times. Driving through the darkness with the window down was pleasant. There had been rain, but now it was fine and the air was fresh. The night sky had patches of cloud that obscured the stars and turned from black to silver when they crossed the floating path of the gibbous moon. I drove on down the wet, winding greyness of the road, the car's dipped headlights flashing across the dark trunks of trees at the bends. The drive to the Ragas house was merely a narrow strip of ungated gravel, that left the road at right angles. I drove for a hundred yards past it then parked the car just off the road next to a field gate. I got out and walked back. The drive seemed long and it took several turns before opening into a large shale forecourt in front of the white house. For a few seconds I hesitated but there was no sign of light or life. An upstairs window gleamed in reflection of the moonlight. I made my way around the side of the house and found the french window without difficulty. It seemed closed but when I pushed, it opened with the slightest of squeaks.

I stepped inside and was in a lushly carpeted corridor-cum-conservatory. The house smelled warm and was very still. I slipped the torch from my pocket and snicked the switch with my gloved hand. After padding along the corridor I came into a large hallway. Another corridor went off in front of me and several doors showed as I swung the beam of the torch around. It was the third from the left, Myfanwy had said. One . . . two . . . three. I paced silently to the door and stopped with my hand on the large and elegant knob. I listened. Everything was still, the only sound being my own breathing. I turned the knob and pressed the door. It opened, rustling its heel on the thick carpet. The beam of my torch came up and hit a wall. I took two steps forward, and the beam traversed the wall flitting across shelves of books and alighting on a desk.

'Looking for something?'

I started violently. Behind me the light snapped on. The man behind the desk looked at me with a lazy grin.

'Maybe a briefcase?'

The thick lips creased the blue jowl in a sardonic grin. Mr Smith was in a humorous mood. I sensed rather than heard the footstep behind me on the carpet, and I was already falling forward when the blow hit me on the back of the head. Probably that saved me from a fractured skull.

Looking back I can picture Smith and the man who had switched on the light converging on my inert body, but then I didn't see anything. My field of vision went black save for a tiny point of white light that grew rapidly and flashed in my face. I didn't feel myself hit the floor.

My eyes wouldn't open. My head reverberated with explosions inside coming at secondly intervals. My cheek was vaguely aware of the softness of the plush carpet. I wanted to stay awake. I didn't know why. The next I knew it was cooler. I was airborne, swinging like a hammock. Something supported my feet. Something supported my head, a head that throbbed. Blackness lapped at my brain. With the ebb came waves of nausea.

Then the vague smell of petrol, my feet dropping slightly, the feeling of something yielding under my body. The slamming as of a door. The sound of another door. Blackness.

The car was moving. I lay still because I didn't want to move and couldn't anyway. Voices murmured. The drive was long. I began to try and make sense, but the effort hurt.

*

A nameless anxiety won and the world became real. I was no longer in danger of blacking out but my head throbbed and I felt sick. I opened my eyes slightly and a pain seared through my skull. The car was travelling. I was lying along the back seat, my feet resting against a large, dark shape. My attacker. Across the bench seat at the wheel was friend Smith. I dropped my eyelids a sixteenth of an inch as Smith spoke:

'He still out Sav?'

A podgy hand grabbed my head which lolled and rolled.

'Yeah. Not much further, eh?'

'No.'

It hadn't been an act. I felt pretty limp. I suspected that if I tried to stand up, my limbs would tremble. And these characters were probably armed. The sick feeling intensified, and a lump rose in my throat. But I lay still. It was all I was fit for. And I couldn't think of anything else to do except lie and gather what strength I could.

Shortly afterwards the car swung to the nearside, bumped slightly as it left the road for the rougher verge, and came to a halt. Smith switched off the engine and turned in his seat.

'He don't look so good does he?' A chuckle. 'Keep an eye on him, I'll come round and drag him out. We'll do it here and roll him down the hill.'

A door slammed, the sound of feet on the gritty road disappearing around the back of the car. My left leg began to twitch in spite of myself. The door by my head opened and hands reached in, groped and gripped under my armpits. Smith began to pull me out. As my knees came level with the end of the seat I tensed and folded, then I pushed off the edge of the seat with my feet, throwing myself backwards with all my remaining strength.

If the ground had been level there, I would now be dead. But the car had been parked on a grass verge at the side of the country road. A few feet further on, the grass dipped sharply and ran down a hillside into trees and bracken.

The lunge took Smith by surprise on the uneven ground. He went over backwards and I went with him, hitting the steep slope, and starting to roll. Smith crashed into a thicket of fern. My feet skidding hopelessly as I tried to brake, I came to a less sudden stop against a tree. I stood up and swayed towards Smith rising slowly from the bush. I let drive at him with my foot and caught him smack on the side of his jaw. Backwards he fell into the undergrowth. I almost stumbled, staggered and stood swaying like a poplar in a high wind, trying to clear my head. A car door slamming brought me round. I glanced up at the road. Silhouetted in the dull, red glare of the car's rearlights was a burly figure. There was a sharp crack as he fired. I dropped like a sack to the ground and pulled myself behind a tree. There was a hush on the hillside. The only sound was the rustle and moan of the wind in the branches.

I crouched behind the tree sweating and trembling. I couldn't think what to do. I lay still. Somewhere, in the damp darkness under the first of the trees Smith was lying. I couldn't see where. Then I heard him groaning quietly as if to himself. Out in the moonlight at the top of the rise I could see the other man.

Suddenly Smith began to thrash around in the fern. He got up and began to flounder up the slope. He didn't say anything. Perhaps his jaw was broken.

'Joe? Joe, you there?' The man with the gun sounded hoarse. Smith stopped and looked around in a drunken sort of way. Then he began to shamble forward past a tree. The moonlight slid across him. There were two sharp cracks together. Then a third. Smith's big frame shuddered perhaps twice, then slumped forward on to the darkness of the ground. Out of sight.

Behind the tree, I was trembling uncontrollably.

Again the voice from the top of the hill. 'Joe.' The big man was beginning to pad down now towards the trees. He came quite quickly, a dark shape I had difficulty in following once it dropped off the skyline.

I picked him up again as his feet crunched twigs. Then he stopped, not five yards away, and crouched over something I couldn't see in the darkness.

I stood up shakily and plunged out at him. I was there when he quarter-turned. I brought my clasped hands down with the whole weight of my body on the back of his neck. His head snapped back. I almost fell on him, then hit him with my elbow just below his ear. He slumped forward across the body of his friend.

I sat down in a heap. For some reason I was near to tears. My head was swimming. Then I rolled on to my front and retched and retched.

For a few minutes I lay there before collecting myself. Sav was still out. I rolled him off Smith, who didn't seem to be breathing. I tried to drag the other man across to my tree but he was too heavy for me. I got him to a sapling a bit nearer where he lay and leaned his back against it. I didn't want him moving too soon. I took the tie from his neck and tied his hands with it behind the trunk. My fingers were trembling again and the knot wasn't very tight.

I sat down, then stood and walked to the car. It stood about five yards off the road, sidelights on, having been driven across a shallow but wet ditch. I thanked God that the ignition keys were in the dashboard. I didn't like the idea of going back down that hill.

I opened the door and sat half in the car. I wanted to go to sleep. I reckoned that I was somewhere between Rubery Top and Lickey End on a back road. If I remembered correctly there was a railway line, or was it a canal, at the foot of that slope. I swung into the big Vauxhall and turned it back on to the road. I had to reverse which wasn't easy, but finally I had it pointing the way we had come. Very slowly I began to drive back to the house.

It was still in darkness and quiet when I got there. I coasted the car, engine off, on to the shale forecourt and made again for the french window I'd entered centuries before.

This time I put the library light on myself and rolled across the carpet to a Claude reproduction showing great vistas of sun and sea. I swung it back and there was the wall safe just as Myfanwy had said. Her combination was right too.

The safe was empty apart from some papers. I looked at them—just figures, cash accounts, deeds, a cheque book. Nothing that looked like formulae. No briefcase. The idea of searching the house didn't appeal to me. For one thing it seemed hopeless. For another I didn't feel like it.

Outside I got in the Vauxhall and drove it back to my own car. Those few hundred yards were too far to walk. Driving my own car was easier. After parking in my drive I went inside and slumped on my bed. I must have gone to sleep fully clothed. When I woke my head was still splitting. I looked at my watch. It was three-thirty—still two hours to dawn. There was something that worried me, something I had to do. I remembered and went for the telephone. I dialled police headquarters, gave my name and asked for CID. A character answered altogether too brightly for the time of day and the state of my health.

I told him that Mr Grey would be interested in knowing where the Sluico drug was being manufactured and I gave him the address of Tarrasch. I said I'd call in the morning and then I hung up.

I reasoned that my own campaign had foundered and that the villains would probably be clearing out of Edgbaston anyway. Better to tell the rozzers before it was too late. Perhaps they could throw a little light on the subject. My oil was running low. When I lay down I remembered something else. Back I went to the telephone and called the police again. This time I went through to the Worcestershire County Police and I didn't give my name. The officer in the information room sounded more decently sleepy this time. I told him he would find a couple of blokes in a parlous state of health if he went for a walk on the Worcester side of the Lickey Hills. I gave directions as best I could, ignored his attempts to get a name out of me and went off the line, I hoped, before they would be able to trace the call. I wasn't able to summon enough energy to really care.

For the remainder of the night I slept fitfully, sometimes heavily as if drugged, at other times just on the verge of consciousness. I finally got out of bed at eleven o'clock and began to consider breakfast, as my stomach felt sickly empty. Someone was still wielding a sledgehammer at the back of my eyeballs. A cup of tea was enough to make me sick, so I gave up the whole enterprise.

My legs were like barely set jelly. I didn't feel like driving. I wrapped up in my thickest overcoat and caught a bus into town. Just before going into the police headquarters I bought the midday paper.

Smith was dead. His chum Sav was in hospital in Birmingham. The police were waiting for him to recover sufficiently to make a statement. They had followed car tracks and found a Vauxhall registered in the name of Savatore—Smith's chum. The road had been wet, the car had left mud on the tarmacadam. The police were now trying to trace another unidentified vehicle which was driven away from a field gate, near where the first one had been left. Bully for them. I hoped they got nowhere.

*

At the central police station I was shown into an office where Grey was already seated behind a desk. Inspector Bland of the Narcotics Squad sat near him. Grey looked pretty pleased with himself as far as anyone with his lugubrious cast of features can do. He indicated a high-backed chair in front of the desk and I sat down. I put the paper on his desk and rapped a headline with my finger.

'Rum do this, eh?'

He glanced at it. 'Still it's on the county's patch and not mine.'

'Have they got any ideas?'

'Fatal gun belonged to the fellow tied up and his prints were the only ones on it. They don't know how the fellow who made it away with the car fits in yet. Why, was it your father?'

I smiled deprecatingly.

'Don't think the old boy's up to it.'

'Doesn't look as if you are either. Had a night on the tiles?'

'No. I think I'm sickening for something.'

Grey decided the pleasantries had lasted long enough. I must have looked as bad as I felt and it was plain that intrigued him, but he switched the conversation to drugs. Even in a playful mood he wasn't all that playful.

'We got your message last night Mr Daly. It confirmed a line we have been working on.'

'Did you find anything at the house?'

'Not a thing.' I bit my lip. I'd held out too long, but Grey didn't seem to mind. He went on:

'We know who the tenant of the house was. He slipped the net on this occasion but we've put out a country-wide broadcast and I think we'll have him within a few hours. We've a shrewd idea where he was making for.'

'How did you tumble him?'

'We've got a couple of descriptions. One from the estate agent, the other from a pusher. We had some officers investigating an incident in which some young tearaway had his hand blown to pieces. There was a tall, skinny beatnik who refused to make a statement but said he'd heard the injured gent was in some new drugs racket and the "accident" had something to do with that. We had a word in hospital. The fellow pushing had no fight left in him and he gave a description that tallied with the estate agent's. Seems the man who was renting this house under the name Edwards is a London character with form for this sort of thing. He's used the alias before.'

I nodded. 'What about his mates?'

'No leads there. We'll just hope he talks when we get him.'

I smiled. 'Well, I've said it before, you'll find the secret of who is behind the whole thing when you find Battersby's briefcase. I doubt if Edwards has got that.'

Now it was Grey's turn to smile.

'I'm damn sure he hasn't. We've got it here.'

The chair rocked under me. In fact I'd go as far as to say my jaw dropped.

'What?'

'We've got it here Mr Daly.' Grey was enjoying himself.

'How?'

'It's rather funny in a way.'

I didn't have much trouble stopping myself laughing as Grey told his tale. It seemed that some constable on the beat up in E division had seen an urchin playing with a newish briefcase. He'd questioned the boy about it and the lad said it belonged to him because he had found it on the railway embankment at the Hall Green entrance to the tunnel. The officer took the briefcase and back at his district station had found it corresponded to the description of Battersby's briefcase, missing since his death. The case had been locked and the kid had never been able to open it.

'What did it contain, formulae?'

'No. Nothing very significant except a letter from friend Edwards.'

'But, wh... what's it add up to?'

'Well it seems pretty clear, Mr Daly, that Battersby had leaked this drug secret to Edwards, an old hand at such things, who was running the racket and giving Battersby a cut.'

My theories collapsed, without so much noise as a tumbling snowflake.

'Why the hell would Battersby do that?'

'We haven't sorted that out yet. Perhaps he didn't like the way he was being treated by the firm. He had had Thorpe-Winman appointed over him on family connexions. Perhaps he was aggrieved.'

I made a last attempt to salvage something from the wreck of a month's work.

'Who killed him then?'

'A jury said it was William Leverton. I wanted to thank

you for your help and to take a statement about this business. I hope you don't begin to make a nuisance of yourself again Mr Daly.'

I rested my head in my hand and ran my fingers through my receding hair.

'How did the briefcase get thrown out of the train?'

Grey was getting impatient now.

'That jury said Leverton's mind was disturbed. Now I don't have to account for all his actions.'

I agreed limply, said I wasn't feeling too good and asked to make the statement some other time.

I stood waiting for the bus to my flat for a long time.

15

Purple blots hovered on the ceiling at the edge of my field of vision. Occasionally, the blots rushed together and merged in a great violet patch, but when I tried to focus on the patch it split and became scores of rushing blots again. I closed my eyes as I lay on my bed and listened to the steady throbbing in my head. I was nowhere. I'd made every mistake in the manual and a few more that were all my own invention. I'd thought the briefcase was the big lead, and it had led me back to square one. The police had the drug racket taped, but no thanks to me. I'd told about Tarrasch too late and I couldn't admit that now. Then there was Myfanwy. Perhaps she had been on the level. After all the combination of the safe had been right. But if she had decided to back a man like Ragas against a stumbler like me who could blame her? I couldn't even drawn any conclusions about the harsh treatment I'd received at Barnt Green. Men in Ragas's line of business probably fill in snoopers on principle. If the police traced my car, I could even be on a GBH charge.

The throbbing in my head went on. It was not so bad as it had been, but it wasn't knocking off just yet. I thought, perhaps Leverton had been lying.... No, the briefcase was found near a tunnel, and Leverton mentioned a tunnel—the one the train entered when he was in the corridor. That was too precise to be a lie. If the briefcase was found before the tunnel, it had been thrown out before Battersby was killed, perhaps then by Battersby himself. Perhaps Battersby and Leverton had been killed by different people.... No that made no sense. I didn't know anyone with a motive for killing Leverton except the killers of Battersby. Leverton was both a dangerous witness to be disposed of and, thanks to the triangle with Carol Morden, an easy frame for the murder.

I thought about that for a time and then it hit me. So

simple you would not give it a second thought. Whoever killed Leverton had to know about the triangle and who did? Very close friends of both men. Yes, but I didn't know them. The village gossips of Dukeswood. I didn't know them either. One person who knew, was the third index of the triangle—Carol Morden. Feeling better I dozed off to sleep.

Next morning my headache was gone. I felt a little woozy after about thirteen hours sleep and my head still felt thick. I wasn't at my best but I didn't feel too bad, and I went into the office. I had some reading to do. I looked through the back editions of *Birmingham Life*. And there it was. Carol's boy friend now was Gregory Cooper, industrialist.

I rang the firm and checked that he was in. Then I was in my car and going out to the place.

It took me quite a time to work my way up from the porter on the front gate to Cooper's secretary. I told her I had to see her boss but I realized he was a busy man and I would wait all day if necessary. As it happened I didn't have to wait more than about thirty-five minutes before before being shown into the presence.

Cooper was fair-haired. His head was square, his eyes grey and his lips full and slightly pouting. He was impeccably dressed in an unadventurous, executive sort of way and he wouldn't be older than about thirty-one or two. Doubtless he was not without background, but it seemed likely he owed his eminence to a degree of ability as well. His accent was acceptable I should imagine in even the best conservatories. In fact he had a slight lisp.

'Mr Daly is it? You're a private detective of some sort? What can I do for you?'

I ignored the 'of some sort' and accepted the proffered chair. His manner was confident, even condescending, but I noticed he was fidgeting with my card that lay on the purple blotting paper in the holder on his desk.

'I'm sorry to trouble you Mr Cooper. I only hope I

shan't have to keep you too long, but I don't expect so. It's quite important I assure you. I've just got one or two points I want to establish and I think you may be able to help.'

'Yes?'

'I'm investigating a couple of sudden deaths Mr Cooper. You may remember them from the newspapers. One of them was quite sensational, the death of a certain Mr Battersby.'

'Yes, I do remember something about it . . . but really I didn't know the gentleman and. . . .'

'I'll come to that in a moment sir, if I may. The other death was that of a Mr Leverton. He died shortly after Mr Battersby.'

'Oh yes, I knew Leverton slightly from Rotary and that sort of thing. He committed suicide.'

'Well, that was originally believed, but now Mr Cooper there is some doubt about it.'

'Doubt?'

'Yes. Both men occupied positions of some importance in their firms. Mr Leverton was a director, and Mr Battersby was a chief research chemist. Battersby didn't occupy a very high place in executive terms of course, but his job was quite important.'

There was a pause. Cooper looked at me with slight puzzlement.

'I know you would prefer me to come straight to the point. It is true isn't it that you have been escorting a Miss Carol Morden about recently?'

He stiffened instantly. 'Yes, but really. . . .'

'Well, if what I say offends you, you can of course refuse to answer my questions. But it is true that Miss Morden was the frequent companion of both these men.'

'Mr Daly, I really fail to see what you mean by all this. Miss Morden has told me about her past—at least as much as I wish to know. Now. . . .'

'Please hear me out Mr Cooper. I don't know what you

do or do not know about Miss Morden's past. That does not concern me anyway. Nevertheless, what I have said is true. In fact Miss Morden as you perhaps do know was named in Mr Leverton's divorce. . . .'

He made mouth movements, but I went on:

'I wish to point out that both these men occupied positions of responsibility in their firms, just as you do. They both went out with Miss Morden, as you are doing, they are both now dead.'

'Well. Mr Daly, I don't know what your purpose is here, but I may say that whatever you are implying against Miss Morden I take strong exception to it. I have no knowledge of what you are talking about, neither do I wish to know about it . . . in fact.'

'Mr Cooper, please do not get angry without hearing why I am here. I have to follow every possible line of inquiry as you will appreciate, even at the risk of giving offence. Probably you can't help. But you see Mr Battersby made an attempt before he was killed to dispose of something that tended to involve him in a criminal enterprise—a piece of evidence that is. It wasn't the police he was trying to hide it from, it was the people who killed him. I ask this question only because I have to, and please don't regard it as deliberately offensive, but have you been threatened in any way recently? In the time of your acquaintanceship with Miss Morden, has any pressure been put on you in any way?'

His voice was as cold as a Verkahoyansk winter:

'Would you care to frame your question more explicitly Mr Daly, so that I can have the pleasure of suing you for defamation of character?'

I shrugged and rose. His attitude seemed unnecessarily touchy to me but I could have been wrong. Perhaps he was naturally stuffy, and loved the girl or something. Anyway there was nothing else to do but leave. I apologized for annoying him, explained to his impassive face that I didn't enjoy it, but it was a necessary exercise. The secretary appeared in response to an intercom message and I was shown out.

As I drove back to town, I began to theorize madly. It's amazing how many internally consistent theories I was able to construct to explain the deaths of Battersby and Leverton. Too bad that each one of them was an intellectual exercise entirely unsupported by any corroborating evidence.

That afternoon I spent more time on replying to a few letters and trying to pick up the threads of my old business. After all it looked as if I would need some goodwill shortly, but I couldn't really put any heart into it. Perhaps I would see Carol herself tomorrow. Or perhaps Cyril would wangle it so I could get a look first-hand at the contents of Battersby's briefcase.

*

I was feeling pugnacious as I lay in bed the following morning. The alarm had woken me up and I surveyed the length of day before me with irritation. I was sick of this case. Sick of having to crawl, sick of being hit over the head, sick of being threatened and condescended to, sick of being conned generally. I was in no mood to be fooled with any longer. In fact I was going to bust it if it was the last thing I did. I'd had enough of getting nowhere.

The telephone bell disturbed my reverie. I sprang out of bed and went to the telephone. A cool, affected female voice was on the line.

'Mr Daly?'

'Speaking.'

'Would it be possible for you to call and see Mr Cooper some time this morning or afternoon?'

'About what?'

A short pause and that synthetic, impressive voice again:

'It's pursuant to your meeting of yesterday I understand.'

There would be no difficulty at all, I said. A time was fixed.

16

It didn't take thirty-five minutes this time and I was facing Cooper again. He was smoking a cigarette with one leg slung over the arm of his chair. He looked relieved as if suspense was at an end when I was shown in. Then he waved at his secretary and told her she could go, that she should not return before being called and that he was on no account to be disturbed.

She nodded her head and slid out sweeping the door closed behind her.

Cooper indicated the chair I was to occupy. I occupied it and didn't say anything. After all it was his party. He swung his legs to the floor and looked at me pouting slightly.

'This is a very delicate matter.'

I still said nothing.

'It concerns our conversation of yesterday.'

I successfully repulsed a small smile that attempted to swing on the corner of my mouth.

'There is something I may tell you but I want it treated in the strictest confidence. It really mustn't go beyond these four walls.'

I nodded. 'Go on.'

'In view of what you said about . . . those two men. Well. . . .'

His body relaxed suddenly and he shot me a harassed grin.

'Well, look here, I don't know what you know or what you're after but I really can't be fussy if I'm not to keep it all to myself, which right now is a thing I don't feel able to do.'

'What I said yesterday was strictly true. I'm investigating for a client who has reason to believe Leverton's death wasn't suicide. You can see that's reasonable—for relatives for example. Anything you tell me won't go any further without your express permission. I promise.'

He nodded.

'All right. I am being . . . if not threatened, something damn like it. I can't make any complaints you understand, I don't want to. But perhaps you can advise me.

'The fact is that I'm quite fond of Carol. She told me some time ago that she was being threatened because of something in her past . . . a personal matter. I don't know if it was true or not, but anyway she said her blackmailer wanted some information she could only get from me. She didn't really want to mention it, she said. Well she didn't ask for anything outright, but she gave me to understand she was in some trouble over this and wouldn't hear of the police. Anyway what she wanted was a trifle. It could be obtained from technical books and periodicals. It was a detail about something we produce here.

'Well of course I told her. It wasn't really secret and far from important. I gave her the information.'

He gave a languid grin. 'She was very nice to me afterwards. It felt quite worth it at the time. Since then she hasn't troubled me again. She acts as if she's grateful and hasn't asked for anything else.'

He lit another cigarette and offered one to me. I shook my head. Cooper was getting quite human.

'I'm sorry I was so brittle about it yesterday, but of course you touched a raw nerve.'

In silence I nodded. He waited for a moment taking a drag at his cigarette and then went on:

'Anyway it was later that I began to get the telephone calls. They began to demand real secrets which would be of very great importance to our competitors—particularly some of the Yanks or Continentals.'

'Who demanded?'

'Well, that's the point. It's a male voice. I haven't a clue who they are.'

'What do they say?'

'They specify the information they want and make threats.'

'Threats?'

'Yes. They say they know I've given Carol information and that they will disclose this to the board. Only they'll say the trifle I've told her is just a little evidence of some of the lesser of my activities and that really I've been selling the firm out lock, stock and barrel.'

'Would the board believe them?'

'Not really. But it couldn't do me any good. A few influential people will think I'm suspect from then on. You know—throw enough mud, etcetera.'

'Did you tell them anything then?'

'No. I told them to go straight to hell.'

'Has anything further happened?'

'Oh sure. They tried again at the beginning of this week. This time they said what they had over Carol still existed. Not only would they ruin me, they'd finish her social acceptability for good. They said violence against her was not out of the question. Then they demanded more secrets.'

'And?'

'I asked them for time to consider my position. That time ran out last night. I'm expecting to hear any time now.'

Cooper dragged on his cigarette then thrust the remnant into an ashtray, working and grinding it into the glass until the end split and splayed. He was frowning intensely. He looked up at me, his brow still creased.

'Of course I've done the wrong thing in telling you. I hope you'll keep your word. But you seemed to know something. What. . . .'

'Do you think Carol Morden is involved with the blackmailers?'

'Oh God, I hope not. I've got to face that she may be I suppose. I just hope not.'

He shook his head, gazing at a blank wall, and biting his thumb nail. I gave a wry grin.

'Yes. I know that feeling,' I said.

He glanced up.

'Well, you don't have any choice really do you. You'll have to tell the police what you've already told me.'

'Oh no.' He waved a hand in the air. 'Not that. When this happened in the first place I should have called the police and put it in the hands of the firm's solicitors. I've done nothing. If this were to become public do you know what it would mean? It would show that I may or may not have compromised in a matter that could mean millions of pounds to the firm; it would mean that I had definitely failed to jump the right way in a crisis. Whether I'm considered honest or not, my fitness to manage will be doubted. I'm too young to step off the ladder now. Oh no.'

'Do you ever go to the Club Cabana?'

He looked surprised. 'What the hell's that got to do with it?'

'Could have something. Do you?'

'I have been there from time to time, yes.'

I leaned forward dropping my elbow on to his desk.

'Look Mr Cooper. Leverton and Battersby both went to the Club Cabana; they both met and went out with Carol Morden. They are both dead. The first two circumstances you share with them. I don't say you'll have the third thing in common too, but just think about it. It appears you have been blackmailed. Well, that makes sense. My bet is that Battersby at least had the same experience. The police don't know any of this. You have just got to tell them what you know.'

'Hell, what a mess!' He ran his fingers through his hair and over his eyes and forehead. When he stopped, his face had a strained look.

'The fact that you have reported the matter to the police will be a clearer indication than anything else of your honesty. Keeping this to yourself is an admission of complicity. If what you told Carol Morden is as unimportant as you say, you have nothing to worry about. You can always think of a reason for the delay. You were making sure the threats were serious, not a practical joke or something.'

He didn't move or say anything.

'And don't worry about Miss Morden's welfare. If she isn't involved her anonymity, just like yours, will be preserved. The police don't bite the goose that lays the golden egg. They'd give a lot to clear this lot up.'

'What if she's involved?'

'You'll never know until it's too late unless you report this. For Pete's sake don't worry about that. Two men are dead because of this gang. Industrial espionage is not a criminal offence. Blackmail is. So is murder. I can't put it to you too strongly that you must lay a complaint that you have been threatened.'

'I've told you a lot. How do I know what you say is true?'

'You told me because you thought I might know anyway. Let's say I knew a little. Where do you think I found it out?'

'All right, give me twenty-four hours to think about it.'

I remembered Leverton, normally so assured, then so harassed, standing up in my office and saying he was going to the police alone. I remembered that within hours he must have been dead.

'Nothing will change in twenty-four hours, except that you will have another twenty-four hours to explain away. These people are dangerous. Once you decide you're going to fight, you have to do it quickly. Leverton died wondering whether to go to the police.'

'Surely . . . I mean this is Birm. . . .'

'I do not exaggerate. There's the telephone. Ring the CID and tell them you're on your way. Believe me it's the only course really.'

He took about a minute. Then without a word he lifted the receiver and asked his switchboard for a line. He dialled the number himself. I told him to ask for Cyril.

Within half an hour we were driving in his Jaguar to the central police station. A wondering Cyril, detached from some paper work he'd been doing, took the statement. I sat in the same room at the back. I didn't have to point out the parallels to Cyril. I just looked smug, and that was enough. You don't have to hit DCI McClellan over the head with a steam hammer to get him to see the point.

In the corridor outside, I shook hands with Cooper and told him he'd done the right thing. He said he hoped so. Cyril took him aside then and had a word with him. I think I may have scared him with the story about the two deaths. I went back into the office and waited. It was several minutes before Cyril came in.

'What are you looking so pleased with yourself for?' he said.

'Oh give it milk Cyril—you know what I think. Battersby threw out his briefcase to stop whatever you found getting into the hands of his blackmailers. They were trying to blackmail Leverton but his Mrs scuppered Carol Morden too quickly. But they still knew enough to set him up for the Battersby killing.'

Cyril sat down. His face already like a plan of an important railway junction creased still further and he scratched his scalp.

'You do go on. But if I buy it for the sake of argument why would they kill Battersby?'

'Search me. According to your boss, Grey, he was a shady character all round, running a drug racket. Anyway why not ask Carol Morden?'

Cyril ruminated for a few minutes.

'Where's the gaffer?' I asked.

'Oh he's in court at the moment.'

'It's all yours then Cyril. Why not have a word with her?'

'Are you telling me how to do my job?' he queried mock-testily.

'Still we've got a complaint. Nothing against her unless she coughs but we're entitled to ask her some questions.'

He picked up the phone, delegated what he'd been doing and called for a car.

'Can I come, mate? I'll be inconspicuous.'

He grinned, 'You may as well. Otherwise I expect you'll go and uncover a plot to steal the crown jewels on my day off. Come on.'

17

Carol Morden had been around all right, but I could guarantee she had never been picked up like that before, not even in the rain.

She answered the door in a pink housecoat and little else. Her blonde hair shook loose almost to her shoulders. The petulant smile on her lips faded when she saw me. I was an old friend from the Leverton divorce.

It disappeared altogether when Cyril introduced himself. I had the feeling she had been expecting someone else.

'Good afternoon Miss Morden. We are making a few routine inquiries into a little matter, and I think you may possibly be able to help.' Cyril smiled disarmingly.

'It would help if you could come down to the station and help us with this little thing. It's a bit too involved to mention here, and we would appreciate it if you could come with us now. I'm sure it won't take long.' Cyril was as charming as a summer picnic.

Carol was about to say something, but he spoke again while she groped for the words.

'I think you know Mr Daly here.' He put a hand on my arm. 'He's helping with the inquiries too, so there's nothing to worry about. Perhaps you would like to put on a few more clothes. They're rather a straight-laced lot down at the station, and it is a bit chilly today.'

Carol said she was expecting someone. She didn't look any too pleased.

'Good gracious, this won't take a minute. If you come now I'm sure we can clear this up in no time at all. It really would be most convenient all round if you could spare us a little time now.'

She asked us to wait in the hall, closing the door quickly in case the neighbours started taking an interest. Not that the glamorous Miss Morden took much notice of gossip.

In a few moments she came down wearing a smart tweed coat over a sober two-piece.

'Has someone reported me for parking again? I'm the world's worst motorist. There are so many silly laws.'

Cyril was still smiling. 'We don't want to discuss it here, do we? I'm sure we can clear it up in no time at all, and the station's only round the corner.'

He ushered the girl out to the car. Walking behind them I couldn't help noticing that she had beautiful legs.

It was only a short drive to Castlebridge police station. Cyril was smoking his pipe and talking about his garden like a benign uncle chatting to a favourite niece. Carol Morden couldn't get a word in. The police station was a new, red-brick building set back from the road. We went through the main doors and Cyril asked a policewoman in the charge office to take Miss Morden through to the interview room.

'I won't be a minute Miss Morden. Make yourself comfortable and have a cup of tea while I get the papers sorted out. This job is all routine, you know. It's as bad as the Civil Service.'

Carol was looking a little edgy when she went out of the office. Cyril turned to the desk constable. 'Inspector Miles here yet? Get him to come up will you.'

The officer left us alone in the charge room.

'Look Max, I could get broken to traffic warden for doing this. If the Chief or Grey get to hear about it I'm going to carry the can.

'I brought her here rather than the central because none of the lads here knows you. But if it doesn't work remember it's my neck on the chopping block.'

I told Cyril he needed a holiday. He was about to reply when Detective Inspector Miles came into the office. Miles was on the city crime squad, and a dedicated policeman. He liked to see the city crime handled by his own crews and took it personally when the regional squad 'pinched' someone on his patch. A favourite story in the police club gave him the credit for breaking up a street brawl between a dozen Irish tinkers single-handed without losing his helmet. But that was in his younger days.

Cyril was talking to him just outside earshot. From his expression I could see Miles was not too happy about having me in for the interview with Carol Morden. Presently Cyril called me across.

'Max, this is Jack Miles. I was just putting him in the picture. We're going to start now. You come in with us and sit in the corner. Take notes if you want too, but I'll have to see them afterwards. Don't say anything. This is a police matter, and we'll handle it our way.'

I nodded, and we went into the interview room.

Carol had smoked two cigarettes and the stubs were in her teacup saucer. The room was small and bare. Chairs were set either side of the desk, one straight and hard-backed, and the other a cushioned swivel. Carol was sitting in a soft, leather armchair to the right of the desk. Apart from the interviewer's seat, it was the only half-way comfortable chair in the room.

The young policewoman sat in one chair with her arms folded. Carol tried to look relaxed. She opened her mouth to speak. Cyril was there first.

'Well now Miss Morden. Sorry about that. I hope they've been looking after you. I just had a few things to tie up. This is Inspector Miles. Would you like another cup of tea?'

Miles didn't blink or even look at her. He walked to the other side of the desk, sat on a chair in the far corner of the room where the girl could see him only if she took her eyes off Cyril who had assumed the interviewer's chair. I sat in the other corner.

She was pretty in a purely skin-deep way and obviously pampered by the opposite sex. This was a new sensation for Miss Morden. She licked her lips.

'All this fuss for some sort of motoring offence. It hardly seems. . . .'

She didn't finish the sentence. Cyril was leaning back in the chair, looking at the ceiling. He moved his eyes to her face.

'There must be a mistake somewhere, or else a simple explanation. How could an attractive girl like you be mixed up in blackmail?'

The word slapped the girl in the face. 'What... what did you say? Blackmail. I don't know what you are talking about. Why have you brought me here?'

Her voice had risen two octaves and trembled a little.

Cyril was the kind uncle again.

'There's no need to distress yourself. I'm sorry if it sounds unpleasant, but someone has made a rather serious complaint to us, and you must appreciate that we have to investigate it fully.

'I think you know Mr Gregory Cooper. He has complained that you have threatened him.'

The petulant poise was slipping. The girl was sitting bolt upright in the chair, trying to control herself.

'Now we just want to know what you have to say about it, so that we can get the whole thing sorted out. You must agree it's not very nice to accuse someone of blackmail without reasonable grounds.'

Carol was about to speak but Cyril raised his hand. 'I'm sorry Miss Morden, but before you say anything there is something I have to tell you first. It's part of the rules, and we have to stick to the rules you know. No one is going to trick you into saying anything.' Cyril cautioned her with an apologetic tone in his voice.

Her voice sounded dull and far away. Her face was pale and make-up stood out in patches on her cheeks. 'I want to see a solicitor. I don't have to say anything. I know my rights. It's his word against mine. He's just a dirty liar.'

'Well now, that's not very friendly,' said Cyril pleasantly. 'I thought we could have a little chat and settle this once and for all. I'm sorry you don't see it that way, but if you want a solicitor, I'll send for him right away.'

He stood up. 'I'll call him myself if you give me his name.' The girl mentioned a well-known city lawyer, and Cyril walked out of the room without another word.

Miles, who had been writing in his note-book walked to the desk. He looked at Carol Morden as if he were seeing her for the first time.

'Come and sit here miss. I need a few personal details for the file.'

The girl rose with difficulty and walked to the stiff-backed chair. 'I won't say anything until I've seen a solicitor,' she said.

'That's up to you, love. Cooper told us a lot and we've got men out checking now. We'll get to the truth one way or another, we're not stupid. It's just a matter of time. They wear grey in women's prisons now you know. Very coarse. Grey wouldn't suit you, would it?'

The girl was frightened. She was licking her lips again, but now her tongue was dry.

'We've got all the time in the world. If you want to do it the hard way, that suits me.'

'He's a liar,' she said hollowly. 'He's a liar. You don't believe him do you?'

Miles leaned on the desk and kept staring into her face. 'Doesn't matter what I believe. If you're guilty we'll get you. Why not make it easy on yourself and tell the truth?'

The girl fumbled for a cigarette and went to light it. Miles reached across the table and took it from her mouth. 'You can't smoke in here. It's against regulations.'

The door opened and Cyril came back into the room. Miles rose and met him by the door. They spoke in low voices so that no one else in the room could hear.

Then Miles said, 'I'll look into that right away. It's in Cooper's statement is it?' He left the room.

Cyril sat down in the swivel chair. He took a packet of cigarettes from his pocket and offered one to the girl. It trembled in her lips and he lit it for her.

'Don't worry about him, Miss Morden. No one at the station likes him. He's a bit of a rough character. I'm afraid the solicitor is out right now, but we're making every effort to contact him. While we're waiting would you like some more tea?'

The girl looked relieved. Cyril sent the policewoman to fetch the tea and she was back with a steaming cup in a moment.

Cyril broke the silence. 'Why don't you get it off your chest? It's better that way you know. Cooper seemed an unsavoury type to me. I didn't like him. He deserves all he gets.'

'He's a liar. I never blackmailed him. We went out together a few times that's all. He's just trying to get me into trouble.'

Cyril looked thoughtful. 'Cooper says you made him get information from his firm by threatening him. He says you would have ruined him if he didn't co-operate.'

'He's lying,' said the girl in the same dull voice.

Miles came back into the room. He beckoned to Cyril and they spoke again by the door in the same low tones.

Cyril left and Miles took the seat. 'Won't be long now,' he said to no one in particular.

The girl looked up. 'What do you mean? Where's the solicitor? You can't keep me here. I want to go.'

Miles leaned on the table again. 'You came here to help us with some inquiries. Those inquiries are not yet complete. When they are, we shall probably charge you, so it doesn't matter if you don't say anything.'

He nodded to the policewoman. 'Keep an eye on her for a bit.' Miles beckoned to me and we left the room together.

*

I waited in the tiny CID waiting room, smoking cigarette after cigarette while the two detectives went about their work of persuasion. It was a slow process.

At one time Cyril would be friendly, inviting the girl into his confidence while Miles played the tough policeman, then after a while they reversed roles. Cyril snarled questions then Miles took over with an air of affable forgiveness. Sometimes they would ask routine questions over and over, making detailed notes in their pocketbooks, at others the interview was more of a chat among friends.

The questioning technique, honed to a fine edge by the two experienced policemen, was designed to break the suspect's concentration until there were no more lies, just the truth.

It was working with Carol Morden. Little discrepancies in her denial of the blackmail allegation were constantly thrown in her face, as the two men made her repeat her story over and over again.

While the subtle torment went on, I waited and smoked. After two hours I was called into the charge office. Cyril was sitting on the desk and Miles stood beside him with his hands behind his back, rocking slightly on his feet. They were both looking at me.

'We can keep this up all night until she cracks. With Cooper's statement we have enough evidence on the blackmail charge to put before the court, and a reasonable chance of the case going for trial, without her admission. If she coughs, and I'm pretty sure she will, then it's water-tight.'

Cyril was talking quietly. We were the only people in the room, but Miles had to incline his head forward to hear what was being said.

'We're going to tell her exactly what is in Cooper's statement, and depending on her disposition charge her now or leave her a little more time to think about it, then charge her. The blackmail case is pretty well made out, but your theories on the Battersby and Leverton killings will go right out of the window. We can't question her after the charge, you know that.'

Cyril was looking thoughtful. He had one eyebrow raised and from the lull in the conversation I gathered he was waiting for my observations on the situation. I was getting some words phrased nicely when he chipped in again.

'I would say she's a pretty scared girl right now. If you're right we could get the whole story. If you're wrong and I start making accusations, then the lawyers will tear me to shreds in court.

'I can explain your presence here as a material witness

in the blackmail case, and I don't suppose I could stop you if you happened to mention something when we go back in there. It's a bit irregular, but not unheard of.'

Cyril stood up and nodded to Miles. I followed them back into the interview room.

Carol Morden was sitting in exactly the same position on the hard-back chair staring at the table top. Her hands were tightly clasped. Miles stood at the corner of the table and Cyril sat down in front of the girl. They both looked grim. 'Have you decided to be frank with us now Miss? It seems you could be in very serious trouble indeed. . . .'

Cyril looked up towards where I was standing just behind the girl's left shoulder. She followed his eyes and when she was looking at me I spoke carefully.

'Battersby and Leverton were both your boy friends. They were both murdered. I think you had something to do with it.'

She jumped up, gripping the edge of the table, her face deathly white. 'You're not pinning that on me. I just did what they told me. They did it. It's bloody Tait you want. I'll have the other, but not murder. I'll tell you what you want to know.'

Her legs crumpled and she collapsed back on to the chair. Slowly Cyril gave the girl the official caution, then lit a cigarette and handed it to her. I exhaled silently—it seemed I had been holding my breath for an eternity.

*

It took the two policemen over an hour to take Carol Morden's statement.

She explained how she had met Lucas Tait at the Cabana, and he had persuaded her to get information from the men he introduced her to. In return she lived the life of a socialite, with plenty of money and a good time. It seemed a small price to pay. Battersby and Leverton were among the names which sprinkled the statement. She had been told of the killings, but not the reasons. She had been told to keep her mouth shut.

18

Lucas Tait was invited to accompany the crime squad detectives to the police station. The wording of the invitation was such that he could not have declined.

He had no form—but for an honest man he had kept strange company.

His interrogation began as a cat and mouse affair but, when he realized Carol Morden had turned Queen's Evidence, Tait reacted in the recognized manner of a professional villain.

He gave the police his story in bits and pieces, adding a little at one interview and remembering a few more details at the next. Nothing was put in writing, Tait was too old a hand for that. At one point he told Cyril, who was conducting that particular questioning session:

'Look, you obviously know a lot about it. I'll put my cards on the table, but don't ask me to make any statements. I've got to have a go and deny it in court haven't I ?'

In police parlance all the detectives got out of him was 'the verbals', but it helped fill in a lot of details.

Tait readily agreed to the girl's story of the blackmail affairs. The victims had been selected at the Cabana, all successful businessmen, and gradually threatened until they parted with whatever professional information Tait required to make the venture profitable.

Leverton had been a difficult fish to catch and he had been dropped when his wife discovered the association with Carol Morden and sued for divorce.

At the beginning Battersby seemed to be just another easy touch, after Thorpe-Winman's talk of drugs, but he turned out to be a bigger rogue than the blackmailers. When the pressure was put on him, he turned the tables, and started demanding a cut of the takings, saying he would expose the racket.

Battersby had to be eliminated, and any of Carol's boy

friends could have been used to fit an eternal triangle killing with a faked suicide to follow. Leverton was the obvious choice because of the divorce. Tait identified Smith and Savatore as the killers.

The police had no difficulty in finding them. Smith was tenanting an ice drawer at the city mortuary, and Savatore was in hospital recovering from concussion and exposure. He had told the police nothing. The riddle of what the two men were doing at Lickey End remained unsolved, and Savatore was not talking.

He didn't change his mind even when the two earlier killings were put to him and he was told that Tait was in custody. But it did not matter, the bottom had fallen out of the bucket.

Tait was charged jointly with Carol Morden on several counts of blackmail. He was also charged with being an accessory to the murders. He had said his piece and had no desire to implicate anyone else. It was suggested to him that someone in a bigger way of business was behind the whole set-up, and Tait's reply was almost classic:

'If I can't swing it with a jury, what you've got on me will keep me inside for a few years. That's not for ever, and I can't swim too well with my feet in a block of concrete. I'm saying nothing.'

A bullet had saved Smith from a murder charge. For Savatore there was no way out. He was later charged and remanded in custody.

19

Ralph Grey was talking to the Chief Constable on the intercom. His conversation was respectfully spaced with sirs. From his tone I gathered whatever the Chief was saying it was not unfavourable to the head of the CID.

Cyril had an expression of pained discomfort on his face, as if his shirt collar was several sizes too small. I was carrying out a detailed inspection of my right shoe.

Grey hung up the instrument after a while and said to no one in particular, 'The chief says it's a good clearance and congratulates everyone concerned. It will look nice in the crime figures.'

He turned to face me, 'You didn't take my warning seriously Mr Daly, but I won't press that any further. It would be a bit pointless, and might tarnish the good name of my department.

'If you were on the force I would have you disciplined for breaking regulations. Policemen who cut corners eventually come unstuck, but then you're not a policeman are you?' He glanced meaningfully sideways at Cyril who was trying to decipher the pattern on the carpet.

Grey was talking again, 'You produced some valuable information, and I'm grateful to you. We are taking steps to have the inquest verdict quashed, and of course the court cases are going ahead and the files have gone to the Director of Public Prosecutions. I feel reasonably confident that we shall get the convictions all right.'

He thanked me again and I rose to leave. Grey told Cyril he wanted a word with him, and I had reached the door before he spoke again. I had a feeling I had been in that position before.

'Oh Mr Daly, you won't go talking to the newspapers will you? All this is *sub judice* and you will be required to give evidence.'

I assured him that I wouldn't speak even to the man who

wrote the crossword and closed the door behind me. Cyril would probably get a roasting from Grey, then a commendation from the Watch Committee. Outside the street was in brilliant sunlight and I walked to my car. I thought I would wait until tomorrow before reporting to Mrs Leverton that her husband's name was cleared and talking about a little payment for my efforts.

I didn't get the idea until I was almost past the off-licence at the side of a new public house. Thorpe-Winman was the only person who had been left out in the cold. He was probably still under cover, wondering what was happening. I walked into the shop and bought a large bottle of Scotch. It was the least I could do for him. Whatever else, he was bound to be thirsty. I stuck the bottle in my coat pocket and finished my walk to the car.

The evening traffic was bad even on the back route I took to Shelly Spires. As I drove I thought about Ragas. There was no hope of pinning anything on him. As usual in organized crime the big fry had taken care to cover themselves, and the police would get no higher in the racket than Lucas Tait.

To my surprise, when I thought of Myfanwy it brought a little pang of regret. I'd had to pretend we were having a mad lightning affair to get what I wanted from her, but the trouble with that is if you say it often enough, you almost believe it yourself. The incident at Barnt Green showed she had either set me up on her husband's instructions or else he had discovered our affair. That was something I would keep to myself anyway.

The flats hadn't changed. I spun the car into a parking space outside the block where Thorpe-Winman lived and took the lift to his floor, the bottle heavy in my pocket. I didn't ring the bell because the catch on the flat door had not clicked home and the door opened as I pressed against it. I wanted to surprise him so I took the whisky from my pocket and stepped into the flat. There didn't seem to be anyone at home. A copy of the evening paper lay on the mat and, down the hall, the living-room door was open. I strode through to the bedroom, but there was no one there either. Then I noticed a small tumbler and a fresh wet patch on the carpet. I bent down to pick it up and found Thorpe-Winman. He was looking straight at me from where he lay under the bed. His eyes were wide and staring but they didn't see anything. Blood had trickled from the corner of his mouth. He was dead.

I shook myself and steeled my hand to raise the bedspread further. Thorpe-Winman's fancy smoking jacket was sagging open. His crisp white shirt was blotched with blood where the bullets had hit him in the chest. I was sweating and the whisky slid from my slack fingers.

I scooped the bottle from the floor, and spent a few seconds wiping everything I could remember touching and some other things as well. I needed time to think.

When I left the flat I made sure the door was securely locked. A middle-aged couple were coming up the stairs, but they stopped at the flat below. I waited until everything was clear and left the block by the front entrance to avoid arousing suspicions. The car hadn't been parked long enough to be noticed, and the evening commuters from the city were not yet home. I managed to control the urge to drive away as fast as the car would go.

The need to be with people was overwhelming. I stopped at a city centre pub and drank a large brandy. The bottle of whisky was forgotten in the car. But I couldn't concentrate there, the hubbub of conversation seemed unreal and the bar claustrophobic.

There was something nagging my mind which had registered subconsciously but had been lost in the shock of finding Thorpe-Winman's body. Something which might hold a clue to his death. I drove home slowly but I could think no better in the car.

The evening sun made grotesque shadows of the tree-lined road as I put the car in the garage and slipped into the house by the side entrance. I had my key ready to open the door of my flat when a relay tripped in my memory, and I remembered.

At a low crouch I hit the door with the point of my left shoulder. It burst open and I threw myself across the room, rolling over on the carpet.

A bullet smacked into the door where my head should have been, and another ploughed into the wall. The dull thuds of the silenced pistol were swallowed up in the room. The long, black barrel was coming round for another shot when I hurled myself blindly at my attacker.

It is not difficult to overpower a woman when you know she means to kill you. The automatic bounced on the floor and skidded across the room. I picked it up by the still-smoking silencer and put it on the table.

Myfanwy Ragas was smiling. She ran her fingers down the side of her face where I had hit her an open-handed smack knocking her from the chair where she had waited with the gun levelled at the door.

She started to get up, but I stepped towards her instinctively, and she leaned back on her hands. The power of speech had momentarily deserted me.

Myfanwy still smiled, and tossed back the black crest of hair which had fallen over her face.

'I'm sorry Max. I don't know what happened to me. Thank God you stopped me. . . .'

I could hear myself speaking. It was like listening to an old gramophone record.

'It was you, not Ragas. It was you all the time. . . .'

I leaned on the table, and she drew her legs under her, rose and walked towards me slowly with the same hip sway which had preceded our love-making. Her voice was soft, soothing. 'We can go away Max. A long way away. Just you and me. I need a strong man. Someone to dominate me. We can go to South America, just the two of us. We can be happy. . . .'

She stopped just in front of me and I spoke heavily, 'You killed Thorpe-Winman and you would have killed me too if I hadn't noticed that my door lock had been slipped the same way as his. When you forced the latch it left tiny marks. . . . Why did you kill him? Why?'

She showed no signs of having heard me. 'They were all so weak Max—weak, crawling little men. Paul let himself get pushed around and squeezed out of Detroit because he didn't have the guts to fight for what he wanted. He didn't even have the nerve to stand up to me so I took over and laughed in his face because I knew he was yellow and spineless.'

She was shaking and the words were tumbling out on top of each other.

'I hate weakness. I hated my father. I hated almost every man I met—but I made them pay. Battersby tried to be clever, and he had to go. Thorpe-Winman talked once too often and I shut his mouth for good.'

She had herself under control again although her eyes were wild. She looked into my face and took a half-step towards me.

'You were different, Max. I thought you were the man I was looking for, but you were only using me and I had to string you along. If only you had left it alone. . . .'

She waved her arm in a gesture of uselessness. 'I came here to kill you . . . after everything we had meant to each other. I must have been out of my mind, and I'm truly glad you stopped me.

'Forgive me, Max. We can start again a long way away. I have money and I promise you I won't disappoint you.'

She was close to me now. If I reached out, I could have touched her, but instead I picked up the telephone and put the receiver on the table.

'You fooled me before and you're trying to do it again, this time to put a bullet in my back. I'm going to call the police Myfanwy. You need help—you're ill.'

I was standing between her and the gun so that she couldn't reach it. I dialled nine, and as the clicking stopped she said, 'How can you believe that, Max? Is there nothing left? Don't you want me any more? Have you forgotten so soon . . . ?'

She looked more beautiful than I had ever seen her before, and a choking sensation in my throat threatened to strangle me. I dialled another nine.

'We could go wherever you want. Anywhere in the world. I have more money than we could spend in a lifetime Max. Oh please Max. I need you so much. . . .'

For one moment I started thinking about her lying beside me on a sun-drenched beach, swimming together in a flawless ocean; speeding through romantic countryside in a fast open car, with her hair streaming and her laughter ringing in the wind; making love on an enormous snow-white bed. The mental images ran on and on. . . .

I dialled the final nine.

JUN 11
AUG 10